A Beautiful Loan

Also by Mary Costello

The China Factory
Academy Street
The River Capture
Barcelona

A Beautiful Loan

Mary
Costello

CANONGATE

First published in Great Britain in 2026
by Canongate Books Ltd, 14 High Street, Edinburgh EH1 1TE

canongate.co.uk

1

Copyright © Mary Costello, 2026

The right of Mary Costello to be identified as the
author of this work has been asserted by her in accordance
with the Copyright, Designs and Patents Act 1988

This is a work of fiction. It is not based on real events, people or places. Any
resemblance to actual persons or events is entirely coincidental.

Canongate supports copyright, which exists to encourage creativity by making sure
that authors, artists and other creative people can be fairly rewarded for their work.
Copyright allows authors control over the use and reproduction of their work. No
part of this book may be used or reproduced in any manner for the purpose of
training artificial intelligence technologies or systems. Canongate expressly reserves
this work from text and data mining (Article 4(3) Directive (EU) 2019/790). By
buying books (as well as borrowing them from the library) you are supporting
authors and publishers and making new and original work possible.

Extract from 'Rivers Grow Small' by Czesław Miłosz From *New and Collected Poems
1931-2001* by Czesław Miłosz published by Penguin Classics. Copyright © Czesław
Miłosz Royalties Inc., 1988, 1991, 1995, 2001. Reprinted by permission of
Penguin Books Limited.

British Library Cataloguing-in-Publication Data
A catalogue record for this book is available on
request from the British Library

ISBN 978 1 83726 310 3

Typeset in Centaur MT 12.5/16.8 pt by Palimpsest Book Production Ltd,
Falkirk, Stirlingshire

Printed and bound by CPI Group (UK) Ltd, Croydon CR0 4YY

The manufacturer's authorised representative in the EU for product safety is
Authorised Rep Compliance Ltd, 71 Lower Baggot Street, Dublin D02 P593
Ireland (arccompliance.com)

For Martin

If you loan to Allah a beautiful loan,
He will double it to your credit
And He will grant you Forgiveness . . .
                                   Qur'an 64:17

Prologue

MY NAME IS Anna, and for some time now, I have been trying to account for certain events in my life – my adult life, that is – which, from this vantage point of forty-five years, I often find baffling. By events I do not necessarily – or only – mean *actual* events or, indeed, specific actions or deeds, all of which are evidence-based and which we might regard as the *historical data* of an individual's life. I mean also that I am trying to understand what went on in my mind over two decades – the miasma of thought, of appetites and instincts, the little tremors of fear or shame; all those inner movements and emanations, those dimly perceived undercurrents that have agency over external actions and events. The climate of the psyche, I might call this, the tropisms of the mind, the subtle vibrations of the soul that affect and, in some instances, determine the outcomes that constitute the historical data. Does man, as Carl Jung believed, draw towards him those outward events that his inner orientation demands? How to understand all this, then; that is my purpose. How to understand why we do what we do, or tolerate what we tolerate, or love who we love.

Part I

I

HIS NAME IS Peter. I can barely hear him above the din in the nightclub. I frown and shake my head and point to my ear and am about to move away when he says something in Irish that I do not fully catch, but which seems to indicate defeat, or retreat. Something a parent or teacher might say before moving on to the next child, something like, Maith an cailín. Whatever the words, the switch to Irish piques my interest, and I reply in kind, in barely adequate Irish.

There follows a rudimentary exchange, half shouted at each other's heads. Cad is ainm duit? Cárb as tú? Céard a thug anseo thú? Cén obair atá agat féin?

And then, Cén aois thú, Áine?

—Nineteen, I say, I'll soon be twenty.

—How can you be finished college and a teacher at nineteen? he asks.

—My mother sent me to school at three – she wanted rid of me.

—I don't believe that for a second, he says.

—Agus tú féin, a Pheadar, cén aois thú?

—Guess, he says, and I guess twenty-six, twenty-seven.
—Close, he says.

After a few minutes, we revert to English. He is originally from Donegal, and retains a touch of that warm precise accent. Handsome too, the more attention I pay, with brown eyes and clear, unblemished skin. Later, I will identify the moment he uttered those words in Irish as the moment that came to shape my life.

My longing to be with him starts immediately, and is relentless. From the pay phone in the hall outside my bedsit in Phibsborough, I dial his number over and over and, finally, he answers. On Saturday night he takes me to a barbeque at his friends' house on the south side of the city. The weather is balmy, and I wear a yellow summer dress and white sandals. In the back garden Mike, the host, tends the barbeque, turning steaks and potatoes wrapped in tinfoil. His wife Alison pours me wine. I try to remember the names: Con and Maeve, Pat and Michelle, Jane, Richie. I can feel their eyes on me. They've known each other for years, perhaps since university. Some of them have children and baby-sitters at home. Maeve has been to a kibbutz; I think this a kind of cooperative farm in Israel, where young people go to work or volunteer. Con says something to Peter, or perhaps *about* Peter, that I cannot catch, and they all laugh. At Peter's expense, I think, or maybe mine. I drink the wine quickly, and Alison refills my glass. Peter moves off down the garden, and I am not sure if I should follow him. I remain alone for a while until Alison returns, and I am so grateful and so nervous that I unleash a torrent of talk and gratitude. But soon, again, I am on my own. I drink more wine. There are lights on in the upstairs windows of the houses backing onto the garden, and I narrow my eyes, like I used to do as a child, until the lights blur and blend and double, and I feel dizzy and drunk. Suddenly I miss home. My father and mother, my sister and brother, will be in the kitchen, watching TV now. Ordinary life there and everywhere, happening without me. Back in my bedsit, the book I was reading earlier lies open on the table. The thought of it makes me less lonely. It has a black cover with a purple vertical stripe – and is not so much a book, I think now, as some gently living thing. *Poems 1955-1959 and An Essay in Autobiography*. There is a photograph of the author, Boris Pasternak, on the front cover; he is wearing a belted overcoat and a cap, and he looks so ordinary, so rural – like the men I know from home, even like my father. He has an anguished look on his face, and he holds his hand to his heart as if he is pleading or appealing to someone. I know he has suffered. One night, years ago, long before I knew who Boris Pasternak was, my father and I watched *Doctor Zhivago* on TV. It was late and my brother and sister were in bed and my mother was moving around the house, absorbed in her chores. My father and I forgot each other for a long time, and then, towards the end, I looked over at him and there were tears running down his face.

I wake up in Peter's bed, my yellow dress bunched around my waist. Instantly, I know. I can feel the pain. I close my eyes, then reopen them, hoping for a different reality. He is asleep on the other side of the bed. In slow, silent motion, I reach under the duvet and pull my dress down. I remember nothing, or almost nothing, but I am sore. And sick and panicked at the realisation of what has happened. I slide out of the bed and crouch down and find my underwear under the duvet, then tiptoe unsteadily out of the room. In the bathroom, I begin to shake, and then vomit. My head is pounding. I cross the landing to another room in this strange house and get into a bed with no sheets. I cannot stop this shaking, or the rapid beating of my heart. I press my thighs together to ease the pain. Outside, it is Sunday morning. The street is quiet. After a while, a car starts up, and children come out to play. I turn and face the wall.

Then I feel him coming into the room.

—What's wrong? he asks.

I cannot look at him.

— Are you upset?

Mortified, and still facing the wall, I tell him.

—I'm sorry, he says. I didn't know.

When I turn around, I see he is naked, and I turn to the wall again.

—I didn't want to do that, I say. I might get pregnant.

—I didn't come, he says, and I hold my breath and say nothing, because I do not really know what he means.

He says those words again, later, when he drives me back across the city to my bedsit. He was not a virgin. I am so stupid. There must be very few virgins left, I think.

—There's nothing to worry about, he says. I didn't come. And then, Are you sore?

I cannot eat or sleep; I am paralysed with fear. Last year, a fifteen-year-old girl died giving birth alone in a churchyard. Her baby died too. The whole country knew about it. I cannot call home; my mother will know from my voice that something is wrong. Or Kathy, my closest friend, because she has never had sex with Seán, her boyfriend. There are nine or ten days left in my cycle. In three weeks' time, I will start my first job, teaching sixth class in a primary school in the west of the city. Now, the excitement and anticipation of that new life is ruined. Everything is ruined. If I am pregnant, it will be the end of the world. Worse maybe than death. I cannot say the word *drunk*, or bear to think of that night, so great is my shame. I had imagined a different kind of giving, an occasion of love, of love-making. *Not this. Not this.* But it is my own fault. I did it, I gave myself to him. I lie on my bed, going over everything. This has to mean something, *he* has to mean something. I have to make it mean something. I get up and go to the payphone in the hall and call him.

I go to the bathroom ten times every hour to check. I go to the church every day and pray, until, finally, the danger has passed.
—I told you, Peter says when I call him, jubilant, that night. I told you there was nothing to worry about.

He drops by, sporadically, after work. I never know when he's coming, so I stay in after school every evening, afraid even to go to the shops in case I miss him. My heart jumps when the doorbell rings and there he is, in his suit and tie, tall and lean and narrow, with long legs and not an ounce of fat on him, the kind of body I will always love in a man. Brown-eyed, dark-haired, clear-skinned. I would like us to go out, do normal things together. I would like to cook dinner, but he never stays long enough, and I'm certain my culinary skills and the rudimentary cooking facilities in my bedsit fall far short of what he is accustomed to. We lie on my single bed, and kiss and press against each other and touch each other, like Kevin my old boyfriend and I used to do. When things start to go further, I push him away. But I know it cannot go on like this, that he will not stand for it.

One Friday evening, he picks me up and we drive across the city and do a big shop in Superquinn, and continue on to his house. When I enter, I push through the air in the hall and force away all thoughts of my previous time in this house. I am changed now, I am an adult. Together, we cook dinner; I set the table and make a salad; he grills the steaks and opens the wine. I look around the kitchen, at the yellow cabinets and the patterned floor tiles, and when he turns and smiles and clinks his glass against mine, I see the tree in the back garden and the little shed in the corner, and finally, I feel calm. But when we go to bed and I do not let him go all the way, he grows impatient and turns away.

In the morning, I expect he will dismiss me, but he is his usual self again. When he says, See you this evening, as he goes off to climb mountains with his friends, I am elated.

2

—TELL ME EVERYTHING, I say, I want to know everything. I am lying across his sofa, with my head on his lap. He smiles, strokes my hair, then tucks it tenderly behind my ear. I close my eyes. So this is happiness, I think. I take his hand and kiss it and kiss his arm, his neck, his whole body, I am so filled with longing.

He used to be a radio officer with a big oil company, spending three months at sea, followed by three months on land. He worked on oil tankers bringing crude oil from the Persian Gulf to refineries in the UK. He had his own cabin on these ships, which might explain why he is so neat — his jumpers are all folded on shelves, his shirts ironed, his socks and underwear tidy, in drawers. A beautiful navy uniform with gold epaulettes hangs under a protective cover in his wardrobe. The officers had servants on the ships, he tells me, teenage Indian boys, who bowed a little when they entered and exited the cabin, and called each officer *Sahib*. Peter's boy laundered his clothes, ironed his shirts, polished his shoes, changed his bed linen. Peter sailed all over the Persian Gulf, the Indian

Ocean. He passed through the Suez Canal regularly. The Strait of Gibraltar. Gib, he calls Gibraltar. Around the Cape of Good Hope too.

As he speaks, I map it all out.

—Coming up the west coast of Africa, he says, the natives would swim out to the ship, and we'd throw down bars of soap and shampoo . . . We'd throw down more, if the women bared their breasts.

Now, Peter is permanently on dry land. He went back to university and qualified as an accountant, and works with a large city firm. But I have the impression, from the way he talks about his previous life, that the sea has not left him. He has shortwave radios all over the house. He explains how sound travels, and tries to teach me Morse code. He goes to sleep at night listening to the shipping forecast on the BBC World Service, like he did at sea, and when I stay over, the time pips wake me up every hour. I think the radio helps him to sleep. I think the hum of the ship's engine and the swell of the ocean lulled him to sleep years ago, and the nightly voice on the BBC returns him to that state now.

During the school day, I am absorbed in teaching and for long stretches I forget Peter. Then, for brief periods while the children are working silently, he comes to mind again and, though I try to push him away, I start surmising, wondering where he is at that moment, and who he's with and what he's doing. In the evenings, to take the edge off the longing, I make mental – and sometimes physical – notes of subjects I will bring up with him. It matters to Peter that I am intelligent and well-informed and can hold my own in conversation with his friends. He reminds me of my father's brothers – reserved, professional men, who do not speak often, but when they do, everyone listens. On history and politics, economics and current affairs, Peter is assured and confident, but on books and literature – which are my forte – he is at a loss. There's a dozen or more books on rock climbing and mountaineering on a shelf in his living room, and there's a novel, *The Wasp Factory*, on his bedside locker, with a bookmark in the same page, week after week.

I begin to imagine him at work, on his drive home in the evening, then moving quietly around his house. He does not own a TV. He listens to Raidió na Gaeltachta at night, to the local news of his Donegal region, then to traditional music and sean-nós singing. There's something in the plaintive sound of sean-nós that reaches him in a way I do not understand, something far-off and lonely that must remind him of the sea.

By Friday evening, I am sick with waiting and the ache to be with him. And then he arrives and takes me to his house for the whole weekend.

One Saturday morning, after he has left for a hike, I open his wardrobe and stare at his clothes. I bring a jumper to my face and inhale his smell, and then start to rummage. High up, at the back of a shelf, I find photographs and a little black velvet box with an engagement ring inside. My heart sinks. I try the ring on; it's too small. I hold it up to the light and see there's a hair, a small dark hair, caught in one of the claws. I rifle through the photos. This must be her, the ring girl. Small, with short, cropped hair and a pixie face, grinning cheekily into the camera. On the side of a mountain, with the sea far off in the background. On a beach with a younger, tanned Peter. With friends in a restaurant, some of whom I recognise from the barbeque. I go through all the photos, my heart beating harder. Here she is, resting on a car bonnet, sticking her tongue out. In a doorway, pulling a face and holding up her middle finger in a defiant, rude gesture.

—Who owns this? I ask, holding out the velvet box, that evening.

—You've been snooping, he says, but he is not angry. That, as you may guess, is an engagement ring that was returned to me, years ago.

—What happened?

—What do you think happened? It didn't work out.

I wait for him to tell me it was short-lived – just a few weeks or months – and that it meant nothing, but he does not elaborate.

—How long did you know her?

—I don't remember exactly. A few years.

—What really happened?

He exhales slowly, noisily. Honestly? She was crazy, he says. We were very young. He pauses and laughs. She cut the wires in my car once. And then later hot-wired it, and took off.

How will I ever know him? Know his past, his secrets, know what he wants? Already I know I am too dull, too tame, for him. I will never match this vibrant, crazy girl.

—Where is she now? I ask.

—I have no idea.

When I'm alone again in his house, I take down the ring and the photos and study her face and her body. What am I looking for? Signs that he loved her, left a mark on her, loves her still? She is wearing dungarees in one photo. In another she is squatting in long grass, peeing. There's a dark green tent pitched a few yards behind her, and beyond that, the ocean. She is flushed and sleepy. They have just had sex, I can see it in her eyes, in the tousled hair. Early-morning sex in the small, hot tent, with the waves crashing nearby.

Now, my life exists solely in relation to him. I yearn to know him fully, deeply – I have no other mission. Sometimes, on Friday evenings when he calls for me, I make us coffee, and when he's finished and stands up and I am about to reach for my little weekend bag, he says, Okay, I'm off, I'll give you a shout next week, and in that gut-wrenching moment I am too shocked and too ashamed to ask, Am I not coming with you? Am I not your girl? I search his face and then – perhaps because my downcast look betrays me and he pities me – he says, I'm sorry, I'm going to Kerry hiking with the club for the weekend, or I have a lot on this weekend. But mostly he doesn't offer an explanation. Then he is gone, and I throw myself on the bed and sob, and there is no one to hear me. I spend the entire weekend alone, too humiliated to meet friends or go home, each hour passing agonisingly slow. In my whole life, I have never felt so miserable. No, not miserable, because misery implies something ongoing; a steady, hopeless resignation. This is different, this is extreme feeling, this is being pitched, over and over, into sudden desolation. This is not love: this is torture.

And yet, I have never lived so intensely or felt so devastatingly alive. I sit at the table in my bedsit and gaze at Pasternak's photograph, and then open the book. On November 23rd

1894, Tolstoy and his daughters are visiting the flat of Pasternak's parents. Pasternak is about three years old and has been put to bed, but late that night he wakes to the sound of music coming from the drawing-room next door. His mother, a concert pianist, and two other musicians — a cellist and a violinist — are playing Tchaikovsky's *Trio*. The child is filled with a sweet, nostalgic torment and begins to cry in fear and anguish. When the movement ends, his mother comes to him and calms him and, perhaps, carries him into the drawing-room where the guests are sitting in a haze of tobacco smoke and candlelight. Young Boris was well accustomed to hearing his mother play the piano, so why all this fear and anguish now? It was, he writes, the unfamiliar voice of strings that disturbed him; he had had the sense that these were real voices being carried up from the street through the open window, voices crying out for help. That evening, he believes, marked the end of his unconscious childhood self, and the beginning of his conscious self that, from then on, was awake and active, like an adult's.

As I read, time dissolves and I feel close to Pasternak, continuous with his mind and the state he's describing, and I forget my present self and want to hold this state, this dissolution of time and the self that his words deliver. After a while, I lift my eyes from the page and slowly materialise again. It is dark outside. I see my reflection in the window and tilt my head and recall my own first conscious memory. I was maybe two or three years old, standing in front of the mirror on the wardrobe in my parents' bedroom; when I moved a little to the right and then to the left, a brown object moved in the mirror. I moved again, and the brown thing moved too. I raised my hand — I could see my fingers in the mirror – and I touched the thing. It was the crown of my head, and my own brown hair. Every day, I stood at that mirror and found my crown. Slowly, as time passed, I saw more of my head. When I went up on my tippy toes, the white of my forehead appeared and, as the weeks and months went by, my eyebrows and eyes slowly rose from below. At some point, I became aware of my *self*, a separate being from my mother and father. It was the moment I understood that I was an I.

I look around my dreary bedsit. Where is he? Panic rises and my mind lurches from one terrible thought to the next, arriving, always, at one: the pixie girl. The pixie girl crowds my mind, and I am riven with jealousy.

On Saturday I walk into town and browse the bookshops. I buy *New Scientist*, and a novel that was reviewed in last weekend's newspaper, and sit on a bench in St Stephen's Green. I try to read an article about the hole in the ozone layer, but I cannot concentrate. The weather is unseasonably warm for October – an Indian summer – and there are couples and groups of young people lying on the grass. The sunlight is pale and otherworldly, and the joy of others and the sight of lovers makes everything worse.

And then I see him, on the grass with a group of people, about fifteen yards away. I see the back of his head, his square shoulders, his long lean back, and something like a vice grips my heart. I gather up my things and hurry around a corner on weak legs and stand under a tree. I want to flee, and forget him, forever. But the need is too great. And then, a surge of courage: I will walk by – I will just walk by and act surprised. I will greet him with nonchalant delight. *Hey, fancy seeing you here!* I will say. *How lovely, bumping into you like this! I've just been with friends.* He will see I am a normal person, who has friends, and a life. And then he will invite me to join him and his friends.

So I turn and stride along the path and, as I near the group, the man who I think is Peter turns around and looks straight at me, and it is not Peter, it is no one like Peter, and this non-Peter raises a bottle to his lips and drinks.

That night I call his number over and over, but there is no answer. I can see the phone in his hall, I can hear it ringing through the empty house. Upstairs, his bed, his folded jumpers, the ring inside the velvet box high in the wardrobe. He is out in the city somewhere, and I am unable to seal my mind off and stay separate from him.

I call home, and as my mother picks up, I can hear her saying something to Fintan, my brother. She's standing in the hall, and he's coming down the stairs, probably in his stocking feet. She will be doing her Saturday night chores now – ironing clothes, polishing shoes, making jelly. She is never idle. My father will be watching TV. I miss them, I miss the house, the fields of the farm.

—When are you coming home? my mother asks, and I say, Soon, soon.

The following weekend I am with Peter again, back in his house, cooking dinner and drinking wine and sleeping with him, and going all the way this time, and there is no going back now.

3

I WATCH HIM closely, this man. I study his body, the way he moves. I cannot bear when he leaves my sight. When he re-enters a room, I want to press myself against him. I crave his touch, his smell; I love the way he sleeps with his mouth open, so vulnerable, and how he throws his leg over my belly during the night and pins me down. I do not tell him that he has become vital, that every leave-taking hurts, that every part of me aches for him.

I can barely admit my secret to myself: that I am sleeping with a man. The feeling is primal; another human being has entered me, enters me regularly now. I am petrified of becoming pregnant, but he assures me he is careful, and there is a hint of impatience or irritation in his voice when I fret. As time passes, I am less tense and, during the safe days of my cycle, I relax and desire rises in me. But I cannot stand the smell of semen, and when he reaches into the bedside locker and takes a J-Cloth from a packet and wipes my stomach, I am mortified. He is unperturbed. He sleeps naked and sometimes walks around naked, with not an iota of embarrassment or shame.

—Dear Lord, he exclaims, one Saturday morning after I climax. I thought I was going to have to go next door and get help.

Out in the world on Monday morning, I feel grown-up and sophisticated, a woman. I sit on the bus, swollen and tingling in the aftermath of sex, and meet passengers' eyes with a slight smile. In school I study the faces in the staffroom, my eyes dropping to each body, wondering who else had sex this morning, thinking how easy it is to conceal secrets.

I meet Kathy in town after school. She asks how things are going with Peter. They have met only once, briefly, and I could not tell if they liked each other. I cannot tell her that I am sleeping with Peter. Though we have never discussed it, I am certain that Kathy will be a virgin on her wedding night, as I had expected to be on mine. Sitting in a café with her now, I feel deceptive, a phony. She thinks I am one thing, when I am really something else. We were once the same, Kathy and I, quiet country girls, drawn to each other from the moment we met on our first day in college. We hung around together, all the time. We went to Mass together in the college chapel whenever we had a free midday lecture. One day, while we all waited for our PE class in the foyer outside the gym, one of the girls wrapped her legs around a pole and gyrated suggestively. I'd like to make love to this pole, she announced. Her name was Attracta. She was from the city – cool and hip and uninhibited. Tall, with thick wavy hair and sallow skin, she wore tight jeans and her full breasts pushed against her vest tops and she emitted a sexual energy that confused and intimidated me. I looked away that day. What was I afraid of? That she'd taunt me, humiliate me, invite me to mount the pole and join her in the gyrations? I knew I gave off an air of fear and uncertainty that people like her could detect. I stood close to Kathy. Kathy never drew dangerous people down on her. All Kathy gave off was a neutral, non-judgmental air of kindness.

—There's a job coming up at home, Kathy says. One of the teachers is retiring in the school. There's a good chance I'll get it.

—That's great, I say, but I am lying. If she goes, I will have no one. Seán will be thrilled, I say.

—I was always going to go back, she says. That was always on the cards.

The phone is ringing in the hall when I get in.

—At last, my mother says. I've been ringing all evening. I was getting worried.

—Is everything all right?

—Do you remember Tomás Burke, from Loughros? He was in school with you.

—What about him?

—He was killed in an accident today. The tractor he was driving overturned.

Something drains out of me, as if I've had a power cut. Tomás Burke was a shy quiet boy. In five years, we never once had a conversation and I never once heard him speak. We shared a set of cousins through marriage and though this was never acknowledged, it was there between us, an unspoken bond.

—I thought you'd want to know, my mother says. I went to school with his mother. Lord, they must be in an awful way.

On the crowded school corridors, he kept close to the wall

and let others pass, eyes always cast down. He was as close to invisible as it is possible to be. When we passed each other, we exchanged a little nod and a half-smile. Our mutual shyness and social paralysis never allowed us to say each other's name, or admit to a connection.

—The poor lad, my mother says. It seems he got up after the accident, and walked away. They thought he was fine. But a while later, he collapsed in the house. He must have had terrible internal injuries.

I look around the hall, at the stairs leading to the other flats. Sometimes, late at night, I hear the hall door opening, footsteps on the stairs, the other tenants returning from socialising.

— Will you come home for his funeral? my mother asks.

—I don't know, I say. I don't think I'll be able to get off school.

Later, lying on my bed. I think Tomás Burke was the gentlest, sweetest person I have ever known.

On Saturday night, we meet Peter's friends in O'Brien's bar on Leeson Street. I hold myself up straight and think: I am one of you now. But I cannot break into the group. When I contribute to the conversation, they look at me, then turn back to each other, as if I have not spoken. By the end of the night, I am close to tears. The following Saturday, it is the same. No one says my name. I remain visibly unperturbed, and show no sign of eagerness or desperation. But no matter what I do or don't do, they exclude me, and Peter does not seem to notice or care. I know the fault lies with me: I am a country girl, with a flat, West of Ireland accent. I am not old enough or clever enough for them. Peter, too, is from the country, as are some of his friends, but they have acquired – or perhaps always possessed – a certain social ease and awareness that evades me. Even as I watch and try to learn, I think there is something cold and unyielding in them. There is one man, Tom, who is kind to me, and occasionally addresses me by name. He is an accountant, originally from Tipperary. When he gets drunk, the others ridicule him. When Con announces that Tom wanked in the back of his car on the way to Kerry last week, I am thrown. I have never heard this word spoken aloud. I look to Peter, but he is laughing with the others. Tom, too, is laughing.

Later, Tom tells me that the whole gang went to see the Pope in Phoenix Park six years ago. One million people, gathered together in my name, he says, laughing. They brought beer and whiskey and drank all morning and when people around them complained, the stewards tried to put them out. Tom leans in now and tells me that someone wet their pants, but I cannot catch the name, and then Con comes over, and I am excluded again. I had been about to tell Tom that I saw the Pope in Galway that year, that my parents and I and my brother and sister got up at 2 a.m. and drove in the dark and had to park the car miles from the city and we walked with the crowd to Ballybrit Racecourse. Everyone moving together in the dark, the sound of our footsteps on the road, and something holy and innocent in the air. The feeling of safety and oneness, and my heart bursting with love for my family, for all of mankind. As we drew close to the gates, dawn broke, and I saw a sea of people spread out across the racecourse. When we got to our corral and settled in, my mother took out flasks of tea and sandwiches, and then a great roar went up and a red helicopter appeared in the sky and came in to land.

4

I AM IN thrall to Peter's life, to its details and adventures. He thinks nothing of it, and recounts incidents in an unremarkable manner, like a mental shrug. I press him for more information, and try to conceal my hunger and fascination. His father was a policeman in Belfast and was once shot in the stomach, and the bullet remained there for the rest of his life. He was married twice, and was sixty-seven when Peter was born. Peter smiles when he tells me this. We Gallaghers go on a long time, he says. He has one full brother, and a half-brother from his father's first marriage. When Peter was twelve, his father died. He barely mentions his mother. They lived alone together all through his teenage years. I have the impression of a teenage boy, suffocating, under the eye of an overbearing mother.

—I cannot imagine losing my father, I say, but Peter shakes his head. He wants no attention brought to such matters, but behind the flicker of annoyance that crosses his face, I detect a vulnerability, a tender, hurt core.

—You still haven't told me your age, I say.

—You guessed it, he says.

But I've calculated that he must be older than twenty-six or twenty-seven.

—When did you lose your virginity? I ask.

He groans. Why on earth do you want to know that?

—I just do, I say. I want to know everything, every iota of his past, his existence. He is my first lover, and he will be my last too. I will mate for life, like my father and mother.

It happened when he was fourteen, he tells me. Every summer, a High Court judge – who was originally from Donegal – and his wife and young family arrived from Dublin and rented the little annex at the back of Peter's family house. One summer, they brought a girl along to mind the children.

—An au pair?

—Kind of, he says, but not a French or European girl. She was from Dublin, from the inner city. On the second-last day, I took her up the mountain – there's a small mountain near our house. There was a herd of wild goats there – there still is, actually. You can sometimes see them from the road, grazing on these rocky overhangs, so close to the edge you think they'll fall off.

—What happened with the girl?

—What do you think happened?

—Yes, but how? How did it come about? Who instigated it?

—Who *instigated* it? . . . I don't remember.

I keep staring at him until we both laugh, and he relents.

—How do these things ever happen? he asks. When we got to the top of the mountain – it's really just a big hill that opens out onto a plateau, a dry bog. Anyway, when we got up there, she snatched my cap and ran off with it. It was a hot summer's day. And I chased her and caught her and pulled her down on the ground.

He gives me a look, as if to say, Happy now?

—And you were only fourteen?

—Correct.

—What age was she?

—The same, I think. Fourteen.

I picture them high up, free, and far from the world, lying in long grass, among wildflowers, bog cotton. It is the girl I am thinking of. The rough heather, prodding her thighs. Who removed her underwear? Was it her first time? Did it hurt, like it hurt me?

—Did you see her again?

—No. They left the next day. I never saw her again.

—What was her name?

He shakes his head. I don't remember. Honestly.

Something makes me uneasy. She was a kind of servant girl, hired by the judge or the judge's wife. A poor girl, happy to have earned Peter's attention. Hoping for love, maybe. He planted his semen in her. She might have become pregnant. I look at Peter now. Does he ever think about her, wonder what became of her? He might have a son or daughter walking around the streets of Dublin now.

I cannot bear this bedsit any more, or the dark streets around Phibsborough. I scour the small ads in the *Evening Herald* and find a room in a house-share on the south side of the city, closer to my school, and to Peter. It is a bright, modern house in a small estate. There are two other girls, Marion who works in Bord Fáilte and has charge of paying the rent and splitting the bills, and Romy from Cork who works in a bank. Romy is small and beautiful with lustrous black hair and brown eyes. She is artistic and, outside of work, she wears hippie clothes and cooks with spices. I love her name, and her life. Her boyfriend is in a band called Ton Ton Macoute, and she goes to all their gigs and sometimes sings backing vocals. In the summer, she's going on tour with them. She's going to give up her job in the bank and sell her car. I tell her about Peter and when they meet, I can tell instantly that he is attracted to her, as she is to him, and so I must keep them apart.

When I am alone, I am still, occasionally, troubled by guilt and shame for having sex, for no longer being the good girl. There is fear too. AIDS is everywhere. It is not just gay men who contract it; anyone who sleeps around can get it. I don't know how many sexual partners Peter has had, and I never ask because I am afraid of the answer.

—When you were away at sea, did you have girlfriends here, at home? I ask him one Saturday afternoon.

—Sometimes, he says.

—Did you sleep with them?

—Some of them.

—Were there women on board the ships?

—Of course. Cooks, crew, female officers. Occasionally, captains brought their wives on voyages. Then he smiles.

—What?

—I did have an affair with a female officer, the first mate

– which is the equivalent rank to a vice captain – on one voyage.

—An affair? Why are you calling it an affair? Were relationships between officers not allowed?

—She was married. Her husband was a doctor back in London. She had a ten-year-old daughter in boarding school.

I am flooded with an array of images. Peter and a married woman – a mother – in a cabin on an oil tanker in the Persian Gulf. A husband back in London, a little girl at school far from home.

—What was she like? I ask, trying to sound casual.

—Very English. All the officers were English, or British anyway . . . She was forty; I was about twenty-five then. I used to knock on her cabin door late at night, a special knock so she knew it was me. He gives three or four raps on the table.

—Wow, I say. You've had some life.

—It's not over yet, I hope.

He looks across the room, as if remembering something else.

—We'd be docked at an oil terminal for four or five days, he says, while the crude was loading, so we'd go ashore every night. Someone would have a contact to get us into a bar. These are all Muslim countries – Kuwait, Saudi, Yemen – so they're dry. Or sometimes, there'd be locals hanging around the terminal, and they'd approach us . . . Sir, beer, follow me. Just those few words . . . One time we were docked in Aden and myself and another radio officer followed this guy – an oldish man – through the back streets and laneways, to a very poor part of the city. He brought us into this . . . hovel . . . with a clay floor and cooking utensils in the corner. Almost no furniture, just one candle for light. Dirt-poor. A curtain separating the living area from the sleeping area at the back where we could hear a child whining . . . He got us two little tin cups and poured some hooch. And we paid him, counted out our American dollars. And we had another drink, and another. He kept saying Sir, Sir, and smiling and bowing his thanks. Then he leaned in and said something in Arabic and winked. He called out, and a woman in a coloured headscarf appeared from behind the curtain. His wife. He said something to her, and when she started to remove her headscarf, we suddenly realised what he was offering. We shook our heads, no thanks. Then he called again and a young girl, maybe thirteen or fourteen years old, came out, slow and shy, from behind the curtain.

Peter stops and looks at me. When we didn't go for the wife, he says, he offered the daughter.

—And, I say, trying to sound neutral against the pounding of my heart, did ye?

He shakes his head. No.

That night we go to dinner in a restaurant called Ernie's in Donnybrook. We pass through a little courtyard with a fountain and a pear tree. Inside, well-heeled diners, waiters in dinner suits, art on every wall. I order sole. It comes with lemon butter and a little bunch of watercress. Peter has fillet of beef with morel sauce. There is a selection of warm breads, served – the waiter tells us – with a little pot of tapenade. We drink a bottle of red wine, and after dessert Peter has a brandy. The prices are exorbitant. I offer to pay this time, or share the bill, but Peter shakes his head.

Afterwards, we go on to a party in an apartment on Eglinton Road in Donnybrook. Con and Maeve are there, and Tom, and I make a beeline for him. The host, Ann Marie, is a friend of Peter's who I have not met before. He doesn't say how he knows her and now, as I watch them talking, I think she must be an ex-lover. I am starting to think that every woman we meet is an ex-lover. On the kitchen island, there's an astonishing display of drinks – spirits, wines, liqueurs, bottles of various shapes and colours. Someone suggests Drambuie, which I have never heard of. It is delicious. Then Peter just walks across the room and out on to the balcony and taps a woman in blue dungarees on the shoulder and when she turns around, they hold each other in a long embrace. When they separate, I think it is the pixie girl, but I am not sure. Tom pours me more Drambuie. Delicious, I say, clinking his glass. Thank you, Tom! Tom, Tom, the piper's son. I think I love Tom more than I love Peter at this moment.

Later there are platters of food passed around. Tom pours me a glass of Irish Mist. This, too, is delicious. Irish Mist gets you pissed, Tom says, and pours more into my glass. Peter is near the door, talking to a couple. I leave my glass down and, as I make my way over to him, the floor rises to meet me, and I walk into it.

Then I am in the bathroom – Peter and I are in the bathroom – and I am laughing and Peter is angry and the room is spinning, and I am suddenly sleepy. He is slapping my face and saying Wake up, and Stop it, and Pull yourself together. He runs the tap and splashes cold water on my face. Then we are leaving, he is guiding me down some stairs, out of the building and when a blast of fresh air hits me, I pull away from him and step onto grass and vomit into a shrub. I am aware of the night sky and the stars and that someone has come out and handed Peter my coat.

On Sunday morning, Peter goes out on a hike with his climbing club. All day long, I am fragile, trembling, my head is pounding. In the evening when Peter returns, we cook dinner, and when we're finished, I can scarcely believe it when he announces that we're going to O'Brien's again.

When we walk in, Tom is standing at the bar, and my handbag is sitting on the counter beside him. When he turns around, he winks at me, opens his mouth, and mimes the act of vomiting.

5

I SHOW PETER my new book of Camus's essays with the author's photograph by Henri Cartier-Bresson on the cover. He studies the photograph and turns the book over and reads the back cover. I tell him that Camus writes achingly beautiful descriptions of his youth, and of the landscape and the sea and the light of his native Algeria. I tell him a little about Camus's life, his childhood poverty, his fame, his death in a car crash when he was forty-six. I have never had anyone in my adult life, like this, to whom I want to tell everything.

—Listen to this, I say, it's about his mother, and I read a few paragraphs describing the love that Camus, as a child, felt for his silent, illiterate mother.

Peter listens intently and is quiet afterwards.

—Aren't you the right little bookworm, he says then.

I was about to describe the moment I first became aware of books – the pull of books – but I hesitate, suddenly wary. He will think I am showing off – and I *am*, to some extent. I am trying to impress him, show him my best and brightest self. But I am, too, bursting with the kind of exuberance I felt as a child when I would run to my mother after discovering some scientific fact or making a connection between unlinked elements – bursting with the need to share it. Prone to impulsiveness and excessive excitement, traits I learned to tamp down as I got older and left the safety of family. How calm and modest and level-headed Peter is, in comparison. He has no need to share or impress or convince anyone of anything, such is his self-containment, and nothing seems to disturb or excite him. But there are times too when he is inscrutable, almost unreachable.

Early in the new year, we go to Paris for a weekend. Away from home, Peter is brighter, freer, happier. Walking along the street, he takes my hand, and I feel his height and masculinity even more so than in Dublin. In department stores he brings me dresses to try on, and when I like one, he insists on buying it. In restaurants we drink wine and feed each other forkfuls of food and stretch across the table and kiss. We stay in bed all morning and order room service and make love and pay no heed to time. In the afternoon, we walk by the Seine in the winter sun, stopping at book stalls and antique shops, and our minds are so attuned to each other and our bodies so synchronised that it feels as if we move in perfect unison.

On his way to Connemara for a club hike, one weekend, Peter drops me home and meets my family. My mother has cooked dinner and is bright and chatty, but when we all sit around the table, the atmosphere is tense and uncomfortable. Peter makes an effort to converse – especially with my mother – but I sense that he cannot wait to get away. With other men, my father could have discussed football or hurling, but Peter climbs mountains for a hobby and my father has no idea how to talk to him. It is exhausting. Later, I am angry with myself for having exposed them all to each other too soon. I worry about what Peter thinks of my family, and am torn between care and love for them and shame that they are not more charming, more worldly, more sophisticated.

A few weeks later, Peter introduces me to his mother and brothers, David and Mark, and Mark's wife Aileen, at a wedding in Donegal. His mother is warm and welcoming, a country woman like my own mother. We meet outside the church, and I expect we'll be sitting together later but, at the hotel, we are seated with neighbours and distant relatives of the bride whose local accents I have trouble understanding. Peter keeps leaving my side to talk to other people. After the meal, he goes to the bar drinking with old school friends, and I am left alone at the table, unsure of whether to join him or go over to his mother's table. I go to the toilet to kill time and, in the mirror, I see that my face and neck are red and blotchy – my childhood eczema has flared up again. I feel ugly and long for the day to end so that Peter and I can be alone again. As a couple, we do not function well in public. We are at our happiest in private.

In late spring, Peter goes to Scotland to hike in Glencoe for a week. Before he leaves, he adds my name to his car insurance, and leaves me the car. It is a beautiful blue Volvo. I have only ever driven on the country roads where my mother taught me to drive. At the airport he hands me the keys, and we part, and I drive back through the city, carefully changing lanes, avoiding buses, cyclists, pedestrians who suddenly step onto the street. When I get to my house, I must mount the footpath and manoeuvre the car between the pillars into the little driveway. I pause on the street, then accelerate lightly, but it is not enough to get up on the footpath. I try again, accelerating harder, and the car lunges forward so suddenly and violently that, but for the wide concrete step, I would have slammed into the front door.

I take the car to school every morning. *Nice wheels, miss!* the kids shout. *D'ya rob a bank or what?* In the evenings Romy, Marion and I cook dinner and, for a while, I do not think of Peter. The loss and insecurity that I habitually feel when we're apart is mitigated by dropping his name into the conversation and by the presence of his car outside – simply catching a glimpse of it through the window returns him to me. Romy and I stay up late talking about our lives. She tells me her parents' marriage has just broken up and her family home is being sold. She and her boyfriend are moving to Germany in July.

—I'm giving up work soon, she says, and Paul is going to leave the band. I cannot wait to get out of this country. It's so depressing, it's killing me.

She takes me to a Ton Ton Macoute gig one night, and we go backstage and join the band. Someone passes around cans of beer and one of the guys is packing up equipment and he excuses himself and apologises because I am in his way and he needs to get around me. No problem, I say and smile and we start to chat in an easy natural way. He is about my age, thin and boyish, with a wispy beard. From across the room, Romy winks at me. Later, as we all walk along the street to a pub, she links my arm.

—Colum fancies you, she says quietly. Make sure you sit beside him.

But, in the pub, Colum and I are sitting across a wide table from each other and when our eyes meet and a smile forms on his lips and his gaze tries to hold mine, I think of Peter wherever he is tonight – far from home, in a bunk bed in a highland hostel maybe – and I feel his pull, strong and compelling, and I look away from the smiling boy.

Before Peter returns, I book an appointment at a doctor's surgery nearby. For several months now, I have been bleeding intermittently between periods. I have tried to ignore it, trivialise it, hoping it will go away, but it has lingered, and I am troubled and worried that it is, somehow, connected to sex. Nervously, I describe my symptoms to Dr McCarthy. I say nothing about having sex, and he does not ask.

—Irregular periods, he pronounces immediately, and prescribes the Pill to regulate my cycle.

I sense he knows about the sex, that he is intentionally putting me on the Pill, and I am overjoyed. Being on the pill puts me on a different plane – I am elevated, I have joined the ranks of modern women who have guilt-free sex without fear of pregnancy. I cannot wait to tell Peter.

On Thursday evening, I hoover and wash the car ahead of his return from Scotland on Friday. In the glove compartment I find his driver's licence with his date of birth. He's thirty-five. Older than I expected, but I had already calculated that he must, at least, be over thirty. His body is strong and fit and he does not look his age. I like the feeling of being protected, even guided, by an older man. And his maturity reflects well on me — Peter is clever, he would not be with me if I was not, at least, his intellectual equal.

From the bottom of the glove compartment, I pick up two little airtight packets and when I spot the label, *Durex*, I drop them, as if they are radioactive. I pick one up again and examine it. I have never seen a real condom. Peter has never used one with me, so these are, I am certain, remnants of his old life. Once, he told me about running into a friend of his — a man in his forties — at a music festival. The man's wife had died a few years before, and he was now in the company of a woman. As Peter was leaving the festival car park late at night, the man came over and asked, An bhfuil rud cosanta agat? and Peter reached into his glove compartment and handed the man a condom. I turn the packet over and consider opening it. I remember a phrase from *Ulysses*, in college. A stout shield of oxengut. Or is it sheath — a stout sheath? And the English lecturer explaining that this was a rudimentary condom for, he said, smiling wryly, the spillings of men.

Peter's flight is due at 6 p.m. on Friday evening. After school, I go to the supermarket and do a big shop. I have the weekend all planned — dinner, wine, croissants for breakfast — and now that I am on the Pill, I feel freer, sexier, more worldly. Even the knowledge that there are condoms in the glove compartment — that I have actually held a condom in my hand, albeit sealed in its packet — allows me to imagine myself a different person.

I wait in the arrivals hall, barely able to contain myself. Twice, a man who looks like Peter comes through the sliding doors. And then he is here, and he beams me a big smile, and I run into his arms.

—I brought you something, he says, and takes out a giant Toblerone.

He drives us across the city, and as we approach Terenure, he indicates and turns into my estate and stops outside my house.

—Okay, he says, I'll give you a call next week.

The engine is running.

—Oh, I say. My heart almost stops. Am I not . . . I was going to come over and cook us dinner. I bought steaks and wine, I say, pointing to the back seat.

—Another time, he says. I've a lot to catch up on.

It is useless to try to appeal to him. I get out of the car, leaving the Toblerone and the shopping behind, and walk into the house.

And this is how it goes, this oscillating life. There is seldom a week when I do not experience some lurch, some punch of rejection, followed, a few days later, by a surge of elation. I am never free of him – he has taken over my mind. Alone, I cry. But he does not suffer, he is immune from suffering. Still, I am addicted to him and to these extreme feelings. I have never lived so deeply, so gravely, so intensely, and I may never do so again.

In the middle of the night, a few weeks later, he rises on one elbow in the bed beside me and, in an urgent, desperate voice, says, I love you. In the morning, he makes no reference to this, and I think he must have spoken in his sleep. Never again in our lives together will he say those three words.

6

MY MOTHER AND I are at home in the kitchen. Elaine is practising her piano pieces in the sitting-room at the far end of the hall. My mother tilts her head as if to listen. Elaine is seventeen, and in the autumn she will go to university in Cork to study music and become a teacher. Fintan will, in all likelihood, become a teacher too. All three of us following the paths of our aunts and uncles. No seafaring officers or kibbutz volunteers. Teachers and farmers, that is our destiny.

—How is Peter? my mother asks.

—He's fine, I say. He's in Kerry with his hiking club this weekend.

I imagine him with his friends, rugged men and women with weatherbeaten faces in Gore-tex jackets and boots, tramping over mountains, crossing rivers and streams, then dropping down into valleys and bogs. He hikes alone too. I think the mountains affect him, the way sean-nós songs do. I think he is privy to something in them – their sorrow or lament.

—Are you all right? my mother asks. You're very quiet.

—I'm fine, I say.

I must never reveal how my life is now to my mother. This place, this family, is where I am safest, but I am keeping secrets, I am disloyal. I think my mother senses the separation of my life from theirs, that something has been severed. I am torn, but selfish too, and so desperate that there are moments when I think I would give them all up, I would give my family up, if it meant I could be certain of Peter.

I watch my mother move about the kitchen. I know her mind; I have always been at one with her. At the age of seven I became conscious of this oneness. That summer, she would cross the landing to my bedroom door every morning and whisper, *Anna, are you awake?* And I was always awake, ready to rise and follow her on tiptoe along the landing to the bathroom where, first she and then I, would use the toilet and she would say – again in a hushed tone – Don't flush or you'll wake the others, and she would wash quickly at the sink and dress quickly standing at the open hot-press door and I would do the same, and then follow her down the stairs. Further and further I would move from my father and my brother and sister and my grandmother, and join my mother in preparing for the day. One morning while I lay waiting for her knock, I had a strange, prescient feeling. I turned my head, and froze. Inches from my face, a mouse walked calmly up the edge of the bookcase next to my bed. I kept my eyes on the grey body, the long tail. I could hear the tap, tap of the tiny feet. I knew if I as much as exhaled, I would startle the mouse and it would fall on my face. I was aware of my mother – any second now she would come to my door and the mouse would panic at her knock and fall on me. And then, somehow, something was transmitted, and my mother did not knock, but I felt her calm presence as the mouse continued climbing and disappeared over the top of the bookcase. As if she knew.

My mother was thirty-two then. She ran the household, cooking and cleaning and shopping, and when that was done, she joined my father on the farm. I imagined that whenever she got a few minutes' peace – alone in the car as she drove to town for groceries or farm supplies – she would remember her young, hopeful self. She would have liked a nicer life, a city life like my aunts and uncles enjoyed, with their suburban houses and neat gardens, their leisurely weekends, their foreign holidays. It's all work, work, work here, she'd complain. All day long, I was at her side, or in her wake, or up ahead of her to foresee and forestall problems and to catch before it fell any object or look or emotion that might cause her eyes to tire or little knots to gather in her stomach, or her weary heart to suffer.

I was aware of these things at the age of seven. I was aware of the tread of mice feet and the fear in mice minds. I was aware that my mother's dreams were ending and that with this life, this family, this farm, she was reaching the limits of her world. I was aware of *her* awareness of the end of hope. In her voice and her movements and in the air around her, it was possible to discern delicate shifts and vibrations, emanations that hinted at what love had once promised, and was now lost. In those moments it was possible to discern the quality of my mother's mind.

My father has brucellosis. It is in remission now but, before he was diagnosed, he suffered inexplicable exhaustion and severe pain for years. In summer, with a heavy workload and pressure to get the work done before the weather broke, he would come in from the fields, barely able to climb the stairs, and collapse into a deep sleep for an hour, before rising again and dragging himself back out, pushing against pain and exhaustion to get to the end of the day's work. There is no cure, and only minimal treatment, so that at any time my father, who places the highest value on work, might, to his deep shame, be found in bed in the middle of a fine summer's day.

He is quieter than usual with me this weekend, and when our eyes meet, I know my mother has told him something. More than anyone in the world – more than my mother or my brother or sister – I do not want to cause my father pain. He is impatient and quick to anger when things go wrong – when the baler or the silage harvester breaks down, or when cattle break into a neighbour's farm. But he is fearful too, and sensitive, and I have, since childhood, accumulated a collection of tender memories and images that evoke in me a terrible sorrow for him. For his vulnerabilities, and his unlived life. He is a bright man but he was taken out of school at fourteen when his own father fell ill. From then on, he worked the land to provide for his brothers' and sisters' education, the same brothers and sisters in whose company he is now quiet and self-conscious. Still, I tell myself, there was joy. Summer Sundays when the work was done and we drove to the seaside, and my father took my mother's hand shyly, furtively, as we walked along the promenade. Or at Christmas when they dressed up in their finery – he in his best suit, she in her long, black velvet dress with the white collar and cuffs – and joined friends and neighbours at hotel dinner dances. And winter nights when we were small and he put Jim Reeves on the record player, and stood me, first, and then Elaine, on his stockinged feet, and danced us around the kitchen. And later when I learned to play *Lara's Theme* on the piano and the sound drifted down the hall to the kitchen, he took my mother in his arms and waltzed her around the floor. Those days ended and, in our teenager years, we found fault with him, and all three of us – Elaine, Fintan and I – turned on him, and sided with our mother. We berated him for his impatience, his anger, for his dogged devotion to work. We accused him of cruelty, and meanness. *Slave-driver*, we called him. All four of us. Four against one, that was the ratio.

You need to relax more, his brother, Tom, would tell him, don't take life so seriously. My father would bristle at the tone. Tom, a teacher, took a great interest in our education, wanting us to aspire to a better life, an intellectual life. Afterwards, I saw how my father mulled over Tom's words, how he strove to contain his anger and frustrations, and willed himself to be a better man. One winter, on Tom's urging, my father and mother took up Transcendental Meditation. Every Monday night, after their day's work, they washed and dressed up and drove into Galway. I would picture them getting down on the floor, awkwardly, onto cushions, a farmer and his wife, out of place among city people, doing their best to breathe in and out, empty the mind, meditate. For the rest of the week, my father would rise from the table after his tea, go over to the sitting-room, close the door and try to put into practice what he had learned, try to quieten his anxious, restless mind.

On Sunday evening my father is standing at the front door to see me off as my mother brings the car around.

—Hurry on or you'll miss the train, Anna, he says. He is a consummate worrier — when he takes me to the station, we arrive half an hour before the train is due.

—Bye, Daddy, I say as I pass him. We never touch.

—Mind yourself, he calls as I run down the steps, and there is a catch in his voice.

Later, as the train rolls across the dark countryside, I am again flooded with tender feelings for my father. For his innocence and earnestness, his tired mind, his worn-out limbs. For the cruelty *I* have inflicted on him. *Four against one.* There is a story my mother once told about their wedding day. When the ceremony ended, my father turned and began to walk down the aisle, alone. He left me there at the altar, my mother said. She had to rush after him, hold him by the arm before the congregation noticed. He didn't know what to do, she said. He had never been to a wedding before, and no one had televisions back then, so how could he have known? When she finished the story, my father looked at her, then down at the ground.

As the train speeds east, my mind turns to Peter. I will never have to feel this kind of sorrow for Peter. He will never need my pity. He is supremely confident, self-contained, devoid of self-doubt. Unlike my father in every way. I will always have to weep for my father, but never for Peter. With Peter my mind will be free, free to read and think and endlessly roam its own territory. It is, I realise, why I have chosen him.

7

ONE SATURDAY, TWO years in, Peter takes me to a house viewing. The house, four-bedroomed, semi-detached, is in a quiet cul-de-sac lined with mature sycamore trees. There's a scent of lemongrass in the living-room. The back garden has a cherry tree, a high old wall, and a gravel path leading to a shed. When we finish viewing, Peter talks to the estate agent in the kitchen.

—What do you think? he asks, as we drive out of the estate.

I don't know what to say. I'm confused, nervous too.

—It's very nice, I say. Are you thinking of buying it?

—Maybe, he says. He keeps his eyes on the road. Or we could buy it together.

—Oh.

—I could rent out my own house and we could live together in that one.

My heart sinks. I know what this means. I would be living in sin. And then, when he grew tired of me, he would discard me.

—Or we could get married, he says.

* * *

I do not think of marriage as a destination, or as *the* destination. What I envision is an enclosed state, a feeling of all-knowingness and all-understanding of the other. A life that recreates something akin to my first life, my first home. The faint, hidden movements and sensations, the feelings of unity I've always felt in the presence of my parents and my sister and brother and which are, I believe, the signatures of love. I feel those faint movements and sensations with Peter too. When I try to tell him this – when I try to describe them – he looks at me askance.

—You know these feelings too, I tell him. You do. You feel them, *I'm certain*, when you listen to sean-nós music, when the sorrowful notes of sean-nós reaches you. Or when you're out there alone and the mountains beckon to you.

I am twenty-three and Peter is thirty-eight when we marry. Elaine is my bridesmaid; she has tears in her eyes and a slightly anxious look after the ceremony. Later, during the speeches, Mark, Peter's brother, welcomes me into the Gallagher family, and my father, in his speech, welcomes Peter into ours. Last night, my father – who, I'm fairly sure, has never spoken in public like this – asked my mother for some notepaper and a pen and went over to the sitting-room and closed the door and wrote his speech. He thanks the hotel staff for the fine meal; the priest, who performed the ceremony; the sacristan, the altar boys, the organist and singers. He rarely looks out at the guests, who are all eagerly listening and rooting for him. I think my mother is holding her breath, willing him on. She will have read over his speech last night, and made little adjustments.

—Anna is our eldest daughter, he says, our firstborn. She's very special to Bríd and me, and to Elaine and Fintan. Then his voice falters. Anna is a kind, gentle girl and we cannot believe she's grown up . . . We cannot believe she's getting married today.

He puts his hand up and fixes his reading glasses, and I look down. At Christmas when I announced I was getting engaged to Peter, a look of shock crossed my father's face. My mother, too, was wide-eyed.

—You're very young to be getting married, aren't you? my father said.

I shook my head. No, not really. And we've been going out two and a half years. We have a date set in July.

—July of this year? my mother said, now alarmed. That's very soon. I mean . . . there's a lot to be done to prepare for a wedding.

—Would ye not wait a year or two? my father asked. What's the hurry?

—No hurry. We just want to get married.

—Well, my mother said, looking pointedly at my father, so long as ye're happy.

My father was silent for a few moments. Yes, he said, and so long as he's a good man.

—But we are not losing Anna today, he continues now. We are gaining a son. He turns and addresses Peter. Peter . . . Bríd and myself, and Fintan and Elaine, want to welcome you into the Hughes family. We hope you and Anna will be very happy. And, of course, we look forward to seeing ye down here in the West every chance ye get.

At which point my father smiled broadly, and the guests clapped and cheered.

* * *

—*My husband*, I say to Peter as we drive down through France to the Riviera on our honeymoon.

—*My wife*, he says back. My wife and I request the pleasure of your company. My wife and I would like to book your bridal suite. My wife and I are not happy with this service. My wife and I . . .

We stop off in rural towns and villages and dine in small courtyard restaurants whose walls are overhung with bougainvillaea. Back on the road, dreamy from the wine, I put my bare feet up on the dashboard and stretch out luxuriously and think of the Mediterranean ahead of us, and St Tropez and St Maxime and F. Scott and Zelda Fitzgerald. Now *this* is happiness, I think. To remain like this, forever, driving towards the sea. I am wearing a loose pink dress, and the heat of the sun is warming my whole body and I tell Peter he will need to find a quiet forest road very soon, because I cannot to wait to get to our destination to have him inside me.

We spend our evenings and weekends working on the new house. Peter pulls up the old carpets and sands the floors, and I stay up late at night making curtains. Peter takes charge of our finances. It is decided that I should have a car, so he surprises me at the school gates one day with a brand-new Nissan Micra and advances me an interest-free car loan of £5,000 which, he tells me, I will repay in monthly instalments of £200. He pays the mortgage every month and I pay all other household bills. Soon, with these bills and the car loan, my bank account is overdrawn at the end of every month.

At weekends we have friends and family to dinner – Mark and his wife, Kathy and Seán visiting from Galway, Elaine and her boyfriend up from Cork, and Fintan whenever he's in Dublin for a football match. I try out new recipes — mussels in white wine, potato gratin — and when we sit around the table afterwards talking and arguing, I am proud of Peter's intelligence and the way the others defer to his opinion. We should put off having a family, I tell him, and enjoy these years, this freedom.

At the weekend, Peter goes rock climbing — which he has recently taken up — or hiking, and I sit for hours in the dining-room, looking out at the back garden with its old high wall, my books and notebooks at my feet. I am deep into a novel about two orphaned girls, Ruthie and Lucille, who are being reared by their strange ethereal aunt, Sylvie, in the lake town of Fingerbone, Idaho. Theirs is a fragile, endangered existence, lived outside social norms. Sylvie, once a transient who rode the rails and moved among strangers, is kindly, non-judgmental. She glides over people and exists in a deeper, almost transcen-dental, state. Lucille eventually pulls away, leaving Ruth and Sylvie alone and more isolated. Death is constantly foreshad-owed, but there's a feeling of redemption or maybe grace, a feeling that the world might yet be made whole. As I read, I am inseparable from Ruthie and Sylvie and my thoughts stream across to them, unfettered, free. Their lives and this novel — elegiac, doom-laden — exert a quiet, hypnotic pull on me, so quiet that it seems that the story is being whispered to me by Ruthie.

In the evening, I surface, and look out at the garden. The cherry tree is still there, the gravel path, the high wall, all now with a melancholy air. This is an alternate existence I am living, a secret, glorious life. If I had not married Peter, if I did not have this house and if Peter did not go off on the mountains every Saturday and Sunday, I would not have this life. I want nothing, ever, to jeopardise this existence.

I stand and put one foot in front of the other and step into the kitchen. I switch on the oven, lift out saucepans, place them gently on the worktop. I take vegetables from the fridge and peel and chop them with slow, deliberate awareness, as if I might hurt them, as if I am Ruthie and each small act is all that matters in the world, all that is needed to stay alive. I turn on the tap and when the water flows, it is miraculous. And then I hear a key in the front door and daylight floods the hall, and Peter, standing in the doorway, breaks the spell.

8

—WILL WE HEAD to Galway on Christmas Eve or the day before? I ask Peter in mid-December.

—I'm not going to Galway at Christmas, he says.

I look at him, alarmed.

—Why not? I ask.

—I'm staying here – in my own home.

—But I always go home for Christmas.

—This is your home . . . You're twenty-three years old, Anna, a married woman. You have to cut the umbilical cord with your family sometime. It's not healthy, this . . . enmeshment with them.

It's not healthy – this has become his mantra lately. You've been too sheltered always, he told me during a row last week, too mollycoddled all your life. It's the reason you're so gullible. You've never known hardship – Daddy and Mammy driving you up to Dublin, settling you into college, stocking up your fridge, setting you up with a bank account. I went off to sea, he said, with ten pounds in my pocket and made my own way in the world.

—But they're expecting us, I say now.

He shrugs. You go, then, he says.

—Please, Peter . . . We can't be apart on our very first Christmas.

—Well, stay then. Your choice. It's all the same to me.

His voice is calm and neutral. This is how he fights – or doesn't fight. I am like a child, and my desperation and neediness, in the face of his calm authority, shames me.

—Please, Peter. I would miss them terribly. The image of my father and mother and Fintan and Elaine at the table on Christmas Day fills me with loneliness.

—Please. Can we go, even just for this year? I am begging now. Then the tears come.

But he is unperturbed. He shakes his head and gets up and makes himself tea.

Later, on the phone, my mother goes silent when I tell her. I can feel her heart sinking.

—Ye might change yere minds, she says. Ye might still make it down.

—I don't think so.

—Even if ye were to come down on Christmas morning, she says. Any time is fine, come any time.

—We want to have Christmas here in our own house, I say, closing my eyes. We want to make it our own.

On Saint Patrick's Day, Peter is in Kerry, and at Easter, he's climbing in Snowdonia. The following Christmas, we stay in Dublin again.

Year after year, he is more reluctant to come west at holiday time, or for family get-togethers. Peter is in Wales, I say, or Peter is in Donegal. That's a pity, my mother says. My father says nothing, just looks away. When, three years after our marriage, my friend Kathy announces the date of her wedding, Peter tells me he'll be in the Alps that week, and I have to beg him to change his plans, and he makes a song and dance about it and, eventually, he does. Some years I stay in Dublin, alone, at Christmas and Easter. I tell no one that he's away. I am learning to grow up, and to cover up. I am learning, too, that Peter only ever does what he wants, and that he will always have the final word.

9

AT FORTY-TWO, PETER gives up alcohol and takes up running and cycling seriously. He joins a swimming club and trains intensely two or three evenings a week and starts doing triathlons. He has drifted away from his friends, and we no longer go to O'Brien's. Instead, on Saturday nights, he goes to O'Shea's or Conradh na Gaeilge to listen to Irish music.

— You wouldn't like that scene, he says, when I suggest coming along one night. You don't like crowded, smoky pubs.

After school and at the weekends, I spend most of the time alone, reading and thinking. I recognise in myself a certain contentment in submitting to Peter's authority, and a comfort in the confidence and certainty with which he makes decisions – all of which relieves me of responsibility, leaving my mind free to mull and wander. On a bookshop noticeboard, I read a flyer advertising a lecture on Jungian dream interpretation in Buswells Hotel, and I go along the following week. It is delivered by an American woman, Barbara Cohen, and I am captivated by everything she says about Carl Jung and dream symbols. She explains Jung's idea of individuation – the process of becoming conscious, the personal transformation and growth of the psyche towards awareness, the journey of the self towards wholeness. These words, when I hear them, set my heart racing. I buy Jung's memoir, *Memories, Dreams, Reflections*, and marvel at his life, his intellect, his imaginative reach. After that, I read *Man and His Symbols*. I start to see connections and symbolic parallels in religion, in Greek myth, in Yeats's poetry – in his concoction of a system of spirals and gyres to depict what he thought was the journey of a reincarnating soul. I see how myth, like fairy tales, accommodates great forces for us, and helps sublimate powerful appetites, urges and instincts. I go to another lecture on Jung the following month, entitled *Aspects of the Unconscious*, on the personal unconscious and the collective unconscious, on archetypes – universal images and symbols, patterns, blueprints and behaviours that are laid down and imprinted on the psyche in all cultures and all ages. In autumn, I sign up for a diploma course on Jung run by the American woman and her sister, Marguerite, and every second weekend attend lectures and dream workshops. I am on a quest for self-knowledge, trying to put my finger on something that I occasionally intimate, but which is always out of reach.

When I tell Peter I've signed up for the course, his face darkens, and he says nothing for a while.

—You have this notion that you're different, he says then, that you're somehow special. He looks me in the eye. You're not special, Anna. You're average, and ordinary, like everyone else. The sooner you accept that, the sooner you'll stop dreaming and grow up.

But even as he is speaking, I am thinking of the books I

bought in Books Upstairs on Saturday that are waiting for me on my desk: Robert Graves's *The Greek Myths*; Jung's *Four Archetypes* and *Analytical Psychology* – his lectures at the Tavistock Clinic in London in 1935. I am thinking of the weekend and the Cohen sisters – Barbara, who will take the morning classes, and Marguerite who will lead the afternoon workshops.

Week after week, I am mesmerised by the breadth and depth of the sisters' knowledge, at how thoroughly they understand the individuation process – widening the consciousness, Marguerite calls it – and how seamlessly they can move from talking about alchemy one minute to Borderline Personality Disorder the next. I can see that Jung's approach to the psyche is a unifying, all-encompassing one that considers not just the scientific and the rational, but the imaginative, the poetic and the symbolic too; how he examines every aspect of man – the ego and the self, the masculine and feminine, the shadow, the spiritual, the artistic, the mystical and mythical and transcendental – and all the unconscious forces that influence him.

For the course work, I must read several volumes of Jung's *Collected Works*. When I find the content and images of *Aion* or *Symbols of Transformation* too esoteric or abstract, I turn to Jung's disciples – to Marie-Louise von Franz's *Archetypal Dimensions of the Psyche* and Barbara Hannah's essays on the animus, or her references to the I Ching – the Chinese oracle technique much favoured by Jung.

Little by little, I can see how projections and complexes play a role in my own life – how, for instance, I have unconsciously projected the positive characteristics of my father onto Peter and how, now, I must begin to withdraw them. Even as I know this, I am not sure how to go about executing such a withdrawal.

But what resonates with me more than anything is the concept of the shadow — the inferior aspects of the ego personality that we repress, the dark, negative, even evil side that we split off through cultural and familial influences. *Seeing and accepting our own shadow*, Barbara Hannah writes, *is really a* conditio sine qua non *of experiencing the unconscious, for if we are still indulging ourselves with illusions about who and what we are, we have no chance whatsoever of being real enough to see the images of the unconscious or to hear its voice.* When Hannah was undergoing analysis with Jung, he said to her one day, You know that as an indisputably honest woman, you can also be dishonest. It may be disagreeable, but it is really a great gain.

One Saturday morning when Peter is gone on a weekend hike in Wicklow, I stop into Xtra-Vision and rent out a film, *The Unbearable Lightness of Being*. It is like nothing I've ever seen. Tereza, a bookish country girl, is desperate for an alternative life. And Tomáš, the promiscuous doctor — I can hardly look into his eyes, he is so undeniably real and erotic. He carries Tereza on his feet up the stairs to bed the way my father carried me when he danced me around the kitchen. Everything between these lovers seems portended. They leave Prague, with all its political ills and troubles, for the country. How happy they are away from the city, toiling every day on a farm. When the end comes, and they drive into the dazzling sunlight, and the credits roll, I sit in the living-room for a long time, then stand at the window and look out on the street. The world is all wrong and all beautiful at the same time. I stand there feeling slightly sick. How can I go on, how can I turn around and step back into my ordinary life again?

I watch the film again the next day. Certain images bring me up short. Tereza, with her books, staring at Tomáš's car as he drives away, leaving her behind in her backwater town. Tomáš, opening his door when Tereza turns up in the city, then standing there, chewing an apple and looking her up and down, then saying, *Take off your clothes.* All the words and images that I am greedy to remember – Tomáš's mistress, Sabina, in her bowler hat; the coloured park benches floating on the Vltava; sweet Karenin, the dog, whose death breaks me. If I ever have a dog, I will call him Karenin. I am not interested in Dubček or the Communists' crackdown – I do not care about politics. It is Tomáš and Tereza I want, their love, their erotic life. Tomáš's cruelty, Tereza's suffering. When she sniffs his hair, she smells another woman's vulva.

Later, I go to the swimming pool and hold my breath and glide under water and feel a sharp, glittering pain, like Tereza's.

I buy the novel and read every word carefully. I understand Tomáš better now. I understand his dilemma, what he is reckoning with – the battle in his heart between the weight and responsibility he feels for Tereza and the burden of her jealousy, versus the lightness of the libertine life he has always lived. Tereza might as well have chained iron balls to his ankles. I am struck by the kind of compassion Tomáš feels for Tereza. It is not pity-compassion but co-feeling. *The art of emotional telepathy.* It is what he feels when Tereza, in telling him her dreams, unwittingly reveals that she has rummaged through his drawers and found erotic letters from Sabina. If she were any other woman, Tomáš would have thrown her out for this breach of privacy. But Tereza is so distressed that, in her dreams, she jabs needles under her fingernails to ease the pain in her heart. Instead of throwing her out, Tomáš kisses her fingertips because, at that moment, he himself feels the pain under her fingernails as if the nerves of her fingers went straight to his own brain. I am exhilarated. *Emotional telepathy.* I think Kundera knows me, knows my mind. He is speaking directly to me. He even tells me what he is doing — how his characters come into being, how he first saw Tomáš. *I saw him standing at the window of his flat and looking across the courtyard at the opposite walls, not knowing what to do.*

School during the week, Jung every other weekend, occasional trips to Galway to visit my parents and Kathy — this life I am living now, month after month, year after year, has a rhythm and routine that contents me. I am happiest when I am alone; I have everything my mind needs — silence, books, contemplation. I think how sublime it would be to exist only as a mind. To be done with the body altogether, with the burden of trying to navigate the world among other living bodies. I want nothing more than solitude, nothing to interfere with my thoughts or take up the space in my head.

One night, Peter and I are watching Channel 4 News when the death of Alexander Dubček in a car crash is announced. I have a sudden flashback to the film, to the scenes when Tereza is photographing the police brutality on the streets.

When the news ends, Peter gets up and turns off the TV.

—I think it's time we started a family, he says.

10

—YOUR FALLOPIAN TUBES were blocked, Dr Boland, the consultant, tells me.

I am in hospital, I have just had a laparoscopy. After almost a year of trying and failing to get pregnant, Peter's sperm was tested, and deemed fit and healthy. Copious, jumping around like nobody's business, was the consultant's verdict. Then it was my turn.

—Why? I ask. Why were they blocked?

—I noticed you have an appendix scar, Dr Boland says, which probably explains it.

—Yes, I say, I had my appendix removed when I was seventeen.

—In all likelihood, it was ruptured, and you got peritonitis. That'll do the damage. It's not uncommon.

I frown. I have no memory of my appendix being ruptured.

—Anyway, I've unblocked them now, so let's go from here, a fresh start.

—Will this work?

—There's a good chance. Though the cilia – the little hairs

that sweep the egg down the tube into the uterus – can be damaged permanently. But, in my experience, at least one tube usually works. So, let's be positive. Let's see you back here in a few months with a baby in that uterus.

Suddenly, what I cannot have is what I want most. After school, I walk through Mothercare, glancing at the baby clothes and buggies and cots, furtively studying the pregnant women who roam around the shop with their partners, willing their fecundity on me. Months pass and nothing happens. One night, just before sleep, a thought grows that something in me resists getting pregnant, that I harbour an unconscious fear of having a child.

But two months later, the test is positive, and I walk into the living-room where Peter is watching TV.

—I have tidings of good news, I say.

For a few hours, we are shy and uncertain with each other. In the following days, the reality begins to register and, slowly, joy takes hold: I am carrying his child. The future appears in images: Peter and his son playing football in the back garden; the two of us driving across the country to visit my parents, our children in the back seat, arguing, like normal families.

But, seven weeks in, something is wrong and, late one night, I experience spasms of pain. I can barely walk to the car. As we drive to the Coombe Hospital, the pain eases.

—This can't be right, I say.

The night-time barrier at the hospital entrance is down, but before we reach it, Peter stops the car and lets the engine idle. I can see the light of the main entrance up ahead. I wait for him to move forward and press the buzzer for admission.

—Okay, he says. Give me a call later.

I stare at him. Are you not coming in with me?

He shakes his head. Give me a call later, let me know what's happening.

I can hardly speak. You have to come in with me, I plead.

—You'll be fine. There's nothing I can do.

I get out of the car with my little overnight bag and try to hold myself straight as I walk up the path to the entrance. At the reception desk, I tell the woman about the pain and how far along my pregnancy is.

—No problem, love, she says, and calls for a porter and wheelchair. She thinks I am single, that this is an unwanted pregnancy, that I've arrived by taxi. If I had arrived by taxi, I think, as I'm wheeled along the corridor, the taxi driver would have helped me in.

In the A&E they cannot get a heartbeat.

—Don't worry, the nurse says, that's not unusual at this early stage.

The pain is gone and the pregnancy test is still positive. They put me in a room upstairs to await Dr Boland's arrival in the morning. I climb out of bed and walk down the corridor to the pay phone and call Peter.

—Hey, he says brightly. How are things?

As soon as I hear his voice, I am relieved.

—I'm not sure, I say. I'm still pregnant anyway.

—That's good, that's very good news. I bet it's nothing, I bet everything is normal.

—Dr Boland will be in first thing in the morning, and he'll probably order a scan.

—I'm sure it'll be fine. I bet there's nothing to worry about.

But the next morning, the scan reveals I have an ectopic pregnancy. The embryo is stuck in the fallopian tube. At lunchtime I'm taken down to the operating theatre for surgery. When I wake up in the recovery ward, Peter is at my side.

—I brought you your favourite, he says, holding a Dunkin' Donuts bag and a polystyrene cup with coffee.

—I had a little girl, I say, smiling. Her name is Chloe. But even as I say the words, I know that Chloe is our neighbour's little girl. I know I'm hallucinating. Still, I am elated.

—It was about the size of a blueberry, I tell Peter when we are home.

—Look, I know you're upset about this, he says, but remember it was just a bundle of cells.

I am barely listening to him. I'm remembering the bins used for collecting syringes and medical waste in the ward – yellow, I think, or maybe red? There must be other bins, colour-coded, for the collections of organic matter – for skin and flesh, blood and bone; and from the labour wards, the debris of birth – umbilical cords, blood, foetal tissue. And among the debris in some bin is my blueberry, my bundle of cells.

—The good news is you got pregnant, Dr Boland says, at an appointment a few weeks later. So, keep going, keep trying. But be vigilant too. This could happen again. An ectopic pregnancy is a medical emergency. It can be fatal. A woman can bleed to death if it ruptures.

On the way home, we are silent. It is there in the air between us. *You dumped me at the hospital gate that night, and I could have died.*

II

—WHAT'S WRONG? I ask.

—Nothing is wrong.

—Did I do something to upset you?

—Nothing is wrong, he repeats. Stop trying to create problems where none exist. It's your imagination, as usual.

But something is wrong. Peter has grown increasingly remote and silent in recent months, and the distance between us is becoming intolerable.

—It doesn't matter about that night at the hospital gate, I say. I understand. It was frightening for you too.

I have told no one about the night he left me outside the hospital, and it is a mistake to mention it now. He gives me a cold stare. Sometimes the depth of his coldness and his darkness frightens me.

He goes away with his hiking club every weekend, and I sit for hours at the sliding patio doors in the dining-room looking out at the back garden, going over everything I've done and said recently that might have upset him. I write him long letters. *Everything in my life is predicated on you, Peter*, I write. *Your mood determines my mood, and it seems lately that every day, every hour, is filled with foreboding now.* Page after page I write, but I never give him the letters. I know the effect they would have on him – he would view them as hostile, he would build even higher walls, grow even colder.

One night I have a terrifying dream. It is night-time and I am being pursued by a killer through a huge old house, fleeing along dark corridors past empty rooms, petrified. I can hear the killer's footsteps behind me. When I get to the last room, I close the door. The room is huge and bare with high Georgian windows. The walls and ceiling are made entirely of glass. I can hardly breathe. I watch the door handle turning and run to the window, but it is useless – I know if I touch a windowpane or if I as much as exhale, the glass will start to crack and the cracks will spread and the walls and ceiling will shatter and a ton of glass will come crashing down on top of me.

It is all connected to Peter – this foreboding feeling. I sit for hours, interrogating myself, mulling over everything, trying to figure out the cause. Peter must be worried about something – he might be ill. He might be having an affair. If he is, it would mean he is mentally attached to someone else. I trawl through his movements in recent weeks and months and, though I cannot rule it out, I cannot assemble enough evidence. I start to think that Peter is right, that I *am* imagining this, that I'm looking for problems, that I have too much time on my hands. His criticisms return to me now. His mantras. You've never known hardship. You've had it too easy. *You'll never be happy.*

The course on Jung is finished, but I return to his books now. Reading him brings me comfort, reassurance, puts me back on the path to the private and deeply inward part of myself that I have strayed from, back to the wellspring of joy and the feeling of enlargement I associate with childhood. One night I am reading about the I Ching — which Jung used to explore the unconscious — when I come upon a passage on chance that strikes me. In the modern world, Jung believed, we rely too much on the principle of causality as an axiomatic truth. Whereas in nature, every process is partially or entirely interfered with by chance. The following Saturday I buy Richard Wilhelm's translation of the *I Ching — or Book of Changes*, and study the method of throwing the coins and interpreting the hexagrams. Now, whenever the foreboding feeling arrives, I will throw the coins so that I might determine the essential, prevailing situation at that moment and, if necessary, try and divert fate.

And then, out of the blue, Peter's darkness lifts and the world comes right again. He leaves the accountancy firm and sets up his own practice in a rented office above the local bank. Soon, he is himself again, and we are recovered. And in no time at all, I am pregnant again.

12

WE AGREE ON names: Clara for a girl, Andrew for a boy. When the first trimester passes, we tell family and friends. My parents come to visit, and Elaine flies in from Brussels, where she teaches music and French in an international school. She wears her hair short now, like Audrey Hepburn, and has a French boyfriend. I tell her she is even starting to look French. When Peter goes out for a while and my parents and Elaine and I are together, it is like old times.

I want to take time off work when the child is born, but Peter is against the idea. He comes in one afternoon and tells me there's a new crèche scheduled to open in the shopping centre, and he has put our names down for a place.

—But I want to stay home with the baby, I say. It will give him or her a good start. And we can afford it.

—The earlier a child gets socialised and accustomed to others, the better. I don't want this child spoiled.

—I won't spoil the child, Peter. A newborn can't be spoiled. I'll be breastfeeding and I can't do that if I'm in school.

—You'll have four or five months off for maternity leave. That's plenty of time to wean the child.

I am silent for a few moments.

—Please, Peter, I don't want to leave our baby with strangers.

—They won't be strangers for long. Kids are very adaptable. After a few days, it'll be like home.

After my six-month appointment with Dr Boland, we go to Peter's childhood home in Donegal for a weekend. Early on Saturday morning, Peter leaves to go on a hike, and I have the house to myself. I lie in bed late, resting my hand on my stomach, trying to feel movements. If I listen carefully and concentrate, I might hear the child's heartbeat just beyond my own. In our early days together, I liked to put my ear to Peter's chest and listen to the thar-ump of his heart. I told him that Schrödinger could sometimes hear the heartbeats of those around him.

After breakfast, I light a fire and start to read Camus's *The Myth of Sisyphus*. Whenever I think of Sisyphus, I am reminded of my father. As a young man he quarried out sand and stone from a hill on our farm and hauled it in his tractor and trailer and helped build the local school. I doubt my father has ever heard of Albert Camus. He was thirty in 1960 when Camus died; he might have been out foddering cattle at the very moment on the January afternoon when the car carrying Camus struck a tree on a country road south of Paris, killing him instantly. I have seen the photographs – the car half-mounted on the tree, the back axle, wheels and dashboard some distance away. The manuscript of the novel he'd been working on, *Le Premier Homme*, was found in his leather briefcase in a field after the crash.

I keep reading to the end of the book. Camus is asking the

only philosophical question that matters – how, in the face of our absurd lives, do we *not* commit suicide? I wish Peter was here now. He is out there in the vastness, a tiny figure on a mountain. I want to tell him that, despite its absurdity, Camus comes down on the side of life, and love.

The house is high up, nestled into a hill with a view out to sea. When darkness falls, I switch on a lamp and stand at the front window, waiting for the lights of Peter's car to appear. I listen to each creak and sigh coming from the far corners of the house. As the minutes pass, I grow uneasy. I think Peter is in danger. And then, far out on the water, a light appears and begins to flash on and off. A fishing boat in trouble, I'm guessing, sending out a distress signal. I watch the flashing light for a long time and when I can no longer bear it, I run and open the front door. All around the hillside is dark. I gaze at the flashing light and stay focused on it until I fall into a kind of trance. Then, something gives inside me, something collapses, and a sharp pain strikes me in my belly or my womb, and I begin to shake. And then as quickly as it started, it is over, and I am purged and peaceful, as if I have brushed against danger, just missing a fatal catastrophe. Above me, the sky is full of stars. I look out to sea again, but the light is gone. I step inside and walk down the hall and lie on the bed and fall fast asleep. When I awake, I hear the back door opening and Peter moving about the kitchen.

Back in the city, I feel something dragging at my centre, pulling me down. One evening, we go to a film, *The Shawshank Redemption*, but I am preoccupied and cannot concentrate. I keep touching my stomach, obsessing, trying to detect movement. When we get home, we take tea and toast up to bed. After Peter has fallen sleep, I am seized with a spasm of pain and then it slowly abates. Another wave of pain gathers and builds, and it becomes almost unbearable as it crests and then abates. I am twenty-five weeks pregnant. In the bathroom a plug of mucus comes away in the toilet paper. When the pain returns, I know it is a contraction and I wake Peter. He looks stunned, like a deer caught in headlights. I put on a jumper and trousers. When I ask Peter to get my shoes from the wardrobe, he hands me sandals. The pain is so bad I have to crawl down the stairs backwards.

Outside, in the driveway, the worst contraction arrives. I lean on the car and when the pain peaks, I gasp, and my waters break, and I simultaneously vomit and expel a warm wet mass from my body. I can feel its weight, trapped in my underwear. Peter helps me into the passenger seat. The pain has stopped. It is all over, I know it is over, everything is over. I lean back, keeping my legs wide apart, petrified to move an inch. I can feel the warm mass between my thighs. It is too small to be a baby, and I am sure it is not moving, but I am too shocked and frightened to look, or tell Peter what has happened or is happening, because I do not know myself. At the hospital, Peter runs and gets a wheelchair. In A&E, I lie on a trolley, and when the nurses roll down my trousers and underwear, they fall silent.

They put us in the penthouse suite. The room is huge with windows that look out over the city, and I am swallowed up by its size and the size of the city. When I get into bed I start to shiver. Peter sits on the edge of the bed. Everything feels cold and remote and surreal. We are silent for a long time. Then, slowly, a peaceful lull falls on us, and I put my hand in his.

Sometime later, a gentle knock on the door startles us. A priest, come to comfort us. Peter and I exchange a frightened look, and it is at this moment that the world returns, and we know there *was* a child, and now that child is gone.

At dawn, Peter leaves and I stand at the window and look out over the rooftops. The sun is far off beyond the mountains. The horizon is streaked pink and orange, more beautiful than I have ever seen it. Peter is driving through the empty streets now. Soon he will reach our estate and turn into the driveway and switch off the ignition and sit for a long time before entering the silent house.

Dr Boland arrives at 7 a.m. He sits on a chair at my bedside.

—I saw your little baby, he says. It's a boy. I'm very sorry. What happened?

—I don't know, I say, and when I start to cry, he pats my shoulder.

—You must have been very frightened, he says.

Tears drop silently onto my hands.

—Could he have been alive? I ask.

He shakes his head. No. He had already passed away. He stopped growing some time ago. It looks like he had been developing normally, and then, sadly, passed away. He was very tiny, no bigger than my hand. Would you like to see him?

—I don't know . . . Maybe.

In the afternoon, I am discharged, and as Peter and I walk through the hospital foyer, I glance up at the TV in the corner. Sky News is on, showing images of a massive explosion in Oklahoma City.

13

WE NAME HIM John. We have a short prayer service at the hospital oratory and, afterwards, he is buried in a communal grave in the Holy Angels Plot in Glasnevin Cemetery. Peter's family, my parents and Elaine and Fintan are there, everyone pale and silent. Peter reaches down and leaves the tiny white coffin, which is not much bigger than a shoe box, into what I now think of as a pit. When I turn around, I see my father supporting himself with one hand against a tree.

That night when everyone leaves, Peter and I sit side by side on the bed. Now, I think, now I will tell him what happened three nights ago in the driveway, that the child came then, that I felt the warm mass but was too terrified to look. I am still terrified by the memory. The warm mass had grown cold on the journey to the hospital. What will Peter think? Are you sure the child wasn't alive? he will ask. What if the child had been alive, even for a few seconds? I leave my hand on Peter's.

—I want to tell you something, I whisper.

Suddenly, he starts to cry, and I am blindsided by his tears. In all the years I have known Peter, I have never seen him cry.

I press his hand. He starts to talk, telling me a story about something that happened when he was twelve.

—It was just after my father died, he says. I was an altar boy and after Mass every Sunday the priest would ask us questions. What is the latitude of the Arctic Circle? Name the four periods of ancient Rome? When were the Annals of the Four Masters compiled? He was educating us, you see, trying to better us. Peter pauses and looks at me. I was a good boy — bright and well-mannered, the priest's favourite. When one of the other lads couldn't answer a question, the priest would sigh and say, Tell him, Peter . . . One morning he asked me a question. Where is Asia Minor? I knew the answer. Asia Minor is the old name for parts of Turkey, Greece and Armenia, Father, I said. The priest shook his head, said nothing for a moment. No, he said coldly, Asia Minor is Anatolia, which is in modern-day Turkey. Just Turkey. I was probably frowning when I said, Yes, but Anatolia includes a bit of Greece and Armenia too, Father, I said. I knew I was right, but he just stared at me, his face darkening with rage. I'll never forget it. I had corrected him — humiliated him in front of the others . . . And that was the end of that. He never spoke to me or addressed me after that. And the following September I went to secondary school, so I finished being an altar boy.

Peter lays his head on my lap, and I stroke it. He rarely talks about his childhood, or anything painful. I want to say something, console him, give his story its due, but I cannot find the words, so I continue to stroke his head. In the silence, my mind moves again to the child in Glasnevin. The moment to tell Peter what happened has passed. Tomorrow he will not want to talk about this, or the child; he will not want to visit the grave. We will go on as if tonight never happened.

—We should have taken him home that night, I say, a few weeks later. We left him lying in a cold hospital morgue . . . He died inside me, you know? And I know the precise moment he died – it happened that night in Donegal when the fishing boat sent out distress signals, and I was waiting for you to come home. I felt something that night, I did.

I look at Peter, waiting for him to speak.

— We should have called him Andrew, I say. It was wrong to call him John. That was my fault – I wanted to save Andrew for our next child.

Still, Peter says nothing.

—Could you see the other little coffins when you left it down into the grave? I ask.

—Stop, please.

Elaine calls from Brussels every evening. My mother calls every night. She tells me that time is a great healer.

—Your father wants to talk to you, she says.

My father rarely speaks to me on the phone.

—I hope you're looking after yourself, he says, his voice breaking. You know, Anna, what happened is terrible, but it might have saved ye from something worse . . . Wouldn't it be worse if it happened when he was five, or fifteen?

I do not leave the house for days. I am afraid to cross the street, or drive, or even get into the car. Anyway, it doesn't matter – Peter refuses to take me to the grave. In the driveway,

I walk around the spot where it happened. Peter must have cleaned it when he got home from the hospital that morning. I stand inside the living-room window looking out, thinking: this patch of ground marks the only trace of his existence.

Nothing is essential any more, not sleeping or eating or reading. I see the wounded everywhere; I flinch at the sight of injured trees, Greek statues with broken limbs, Christ nailed to the cross. I ask Peter if he, too, has an awareness of the child's presence around him, and he shakes his head. I tell him I believe in some kind of metaphysical existence, and that I sense it, I sense the child's soul. I want to talk about his physical existence too — when did one organism become two, when did *I* become him and me? A line keeps looping in my brain. *And then the dead was born.* It sounds familiar, as if it is from Scripture, embedded in my memory from way back. I ask Peter if he recognises it. I have a great need to talk, to tease all this out with him. But this is exactly the kind of talk that Peter cannot stand.

In *New Scientist* one morning I read that scientists estimate there are about ten thousand intelligent alien civilisations in our galaxy alone, and the thought of this strangely comforts me. That afternoon I walk to the end of the street, and the following day to the end of the estate. Finally, one day, I walk past the shops and the school to the church, and sit in a pew. I am overcome with grief for the child, for the little scrap of a child inside the white, felt-covered, plywood box. Can I even call him a child at six months' gestation? Did he have any glimmer of awareness in utero? Even a picosecond of consciousness, a brief flickering of mind? I close my eyes for a moment and the enormity of what happened hits me. I was the only person responsible for him, and he died in my care. He, who was sinless, *died in my care.* I am, in some way, culpable. Was it something I did or didn't do, something I said or thought that interfered with his progress or harmed him? My heart starts to race. In my youth, I had a recurring dream that I had committed murder and gotten away with it, and when I awoke in the morning, I was terrified. I feel now as I used to feel then: sick and frightened and not at all certain that I am innocent. I lift my eyes to the stained-glass window, then to the sanctuary lamp. I gaze at the red glow until its warmth calms my heart and the fear subsides. I become rapt, entranced by the glow of the lamp. I am back in the peace of childhood, I am with my grandmother in the church. In the presence of God again. I think: The child is in heaven. If I concentrate – if I close my eyes and concentrate deeply – I might see him, seated at the right hand of the Father. How lucky he is – he will never know pain, he will never have to suffer this world. I am euphoric at this thought, and benevolence spreads through me, and I bow my head and thank God for this blessing.

But as soon as I leave the church, the goodness dissipates, and I am paralysed with fear again.

We meet Dr Boland in his consulting rooms a few weeks later. He is short and round and bald and, when we first met him a few years ago, Peter christened him Dr DeVito. He has lovely white hands. I remember them touching my stomach, palpating it.

Peter starts to grill him. What happened? he asks. Was there something wrong with the child?

Dr Boland shakes his head. Your little boy was normal, he says, but he was underweight and underdeveloped for twenty-five weeks.

—Why? Peter presses. Why was he underdeveloped?

—We can't say for certain, but a condition called placental insufficiency is the most likely cause. It's when the baby doesn't get enough oxygen and nutrients from the placenta. Your baby had been developing normally, but at some stage before he was born, he stopped growing. He was . . . Sadly, he had passed away some time before he arrived, possibly a week before.

So he did not die that night in Donegal, as I watched the fishing boat out on the water. He slowly starved inside me. When they brought him to me that morning in the penthouse suite in the hospital, the sight of him frightened me. He did not look like a human baby. All his limbs were there, and minute fingers and toes, but his skin was the colour of clay, and his body seemed old and shrunken, like an extraterrestrial's. When Peter returned later, he did not want to see him.

Peter pushes harder. Why hadn't he, Dr Boland, detected this problem at the six-month check-up? Had he listened to the heartbeat that day?

Dr Boland is about to speak, but Peter keeps going.

—She was too small, he says, her bump was too small. It was obvious to everyone. Why didn't she have a scan that day?

Please, Peter, go easy.

Dr Boland nods. There was a heartbeat that day, he says. Yes, she was small, but that's not unusual in a first pregnancy. There was no pain, no bleeding, so I had no cause for concern.

His voice soothes me, like it did at my bedside that morning when he asked me what happened, and I said I didn't know.

But somewhere far inside me, I knew. Even then, I knew this child was never deemed. The child himself knew it.

He had said the words, *Your little baby*, several times that morning. I knew the nurses had told him how they found the child, that they had unrolled my trousers and lifted the tiny body from between my thighs. He knew everything about me and my baby, and I felt no shame or blame or guilt. I felt only his protection.

I look at Peter now, talking, talking. And then I look at Dr Boland and I feel a surge of love for him, and I think if *he* were my husband, if *he* had impregnated me, the child would not have died.

14

IT IS MY idea to get a dog. Peter is away in Scotland when I collect the pup from the breeder on a dark evening during the Halloween school break. Rose, a heavy, middle-aged woman, with thin grey hair, leads me into her kitchen where a litter of Cavalier King Charles pups are curled up asleep in a child's playpen. The one I choose is named Glamour Girl on her Kennel Club certificate. Rose lifts her into a cardboard box which I place on the back seat of the car. All the way home, the pup makes no sound. When I ease the box sideways on the kitchen floor, she gives a little whimper and slides out and slips on the tiles.

—Here, here, I say, kneeling on the floor, and she comes to me, and then goes back inside the box.

I lean in and whisper, BOO! She wags her tail and comes out and tries to climb onto my lap. Boo, I whisper again into her ear and, again, she wags her tail. She runs around the kitchen floor until she tires, then sits looking at me until her eyelids begin to droop and her head drops. I sit on the floor beside her, and she climbs onto my lap and curls up and falls asleep, and I am moved by her innocence and trust.

—Her name is Boo, I tell Peter on the phone.

—Not Karenin? he asks.

—No, I say. I can't burden her with that name. She's tiny – no bigger than a kitten. I can hold her in the palm of my hand.

During the night, I hear her whimpering downstairs. Don't give in, Peter had instructed. Start as you mean to go on, don't give her bad habits. But I cannot bear it. I bring her up to the bedroom and she sleeps through the night. In the morning, I take her out to the back garden; her legs are so short and her body so small she has to leap over the grass.

When Peter returns, he insists she sleeps downstairs.

—Please, I say. She wants company. She's missing her mother and her siblings, the little den.

—You'll spoil her, he says. Give her an inch, she'll take a mile.

Defeated, I wrap my jumper around a clock and place it in her bed in the kitchen. When she cries in the night, I go down and sit beside her, stroking her until she falls asleep.

She takes over my life. I feed her and walk her before school every morning, and rush home in the afternoon. I socialise less and less because I never want to leave her. I take her to Galway with me, curled up asleep in the passenger seat for the journey. Sometimes, she lifts her head and looks over, as if to check I am still there. She has altered me, generated in me a new awareness of animal consciousness, of their moment-by-moment existence. I can no longer eat meat. When I pass a livestock truck on the road, crammed with pigs or sheep or cattle on their way to slaughter, my chest tightens. I think of my father's cattle, walking meekly up the chute to their death in the meat factory. This is what Boo has done to me. I start seeing it everywhere, the innocent suffering of animals. Hungry horses standing knee-deep in mucky gateways, cattle gathered around empty feeders, circus wagons and animal trucks parked on waste ground on the edges of towns. I buy books by Peter Singer, Tom Regan, Andrew Linzey, and read gruesome accounts of animal experiments in laboratories. The question is not can they feel, or can they think, but can they suffer?

One Saturday morning when Boo is almost a year old, Peter and I take her to the park. She is fully grown now. She runs off – away from us – to a group of children who make a fuss over her. Peter runs to retrieve her, picks her up roughly, and scolds her.

—*Peter*, I say, go easy.

He has been moody and remote again for months and I can sense, around him, a new field of indifference. He has changed in other ways too – he has let his hair grow and wears a ponytail which is, I think, compensation for his balding crown. Whenever I suggest that we should start trying for a baby again, he says it's not the right time.

One night, in bed, we are both awake, lying there in silence.

—Something is wrong, I say, into the darkness. I can feel it, between us.

—I don't want to be married any more, he says.

He says it again, *I don't want to be married any more,* and my heart tilts and pitches and something like an electrical current sweeps through my body.

—You don't want to be married? I whisper. What does that mean?

—I'm sorry.

—For what?

—I should never have gotten married. It was a bad idea. Marriage isn't right for me.

I wait for whatever is to come next.

—It's not your fault, he continues, it has nothing to do with you.

—It has everything to do with me, I say. I sit up and switch on the lamp. You can't just turn around after eight years of marriage and announce you want out. I can feel panic rising.

He wants the lamp off, but I stay sitting up because if I lie down I will not be able to breathe.

—Is there someone else? I ask. Are you having an affair?

—There's no one else.

—What then? Is this grief, still, over the child? We've been through a lot. I feel it too.

—It's not grief.

—Are you ill? Is there something you're not telling me?

—I'm not ill.

—This is just a bad patch, Peter, I say. We've been through bad patches before. It happens in long marriages. We should take a holiday, get away together for a change.

After a long silence, he says, You should take a holiday yourself. Go to Brussels, visit Elaine.

My heart sinks.

—I don't want to go to Brussels. I don't want to go anywhere without you.

Another silence.

—What's happening? I ask. I can feel the ground shifting. Why are you doing this? There must be some reason. There must be someone else. Is there someone else?

—I told you. I just don't want to be married any more.

Suddenly something occurs to me. Are you gay? I ask.

—No, Anna, I'm not gay.

—But you can't give up on us just like that. We're *married*, Peter. People don't give up on a whim, just because they don't *feel* like being married.

—It's not a whim.

He sits up, so that we are sitting side by side in the dark now. I'm afraid to ask if he still loves me.

—Don't you sometimes feel like this too? he asks. Wouldn't you like to be alone? He turns towards me, warmed to his task now. I'm afraid Boo will hear him downstairs and start to whine.

—That's different. We all need solitude at times. But I don't want to leave our marriage.

—You don't know that. You might be relieved, he says. He has brightened — now that he has unburdened himself, he is energised, almost excited.

Downstairs, Boo starts to cry, but I cannot move. A kaleidoscope of shapes and colours move and merge in front of me, like the aura before a migraine. Something is happening. Something is happening simultaneously inside me and far from me, some kind of fusion. And I have a flash — a vision of particles colliding, an explosion of bright colours and, for a second, I get a glimpse of the infinite suffering in the heart of an atom.

I can hear Boo crying again.

—You should socialise more, Peter is saying. You're still a young woman. Go and visit Elaine in Brussels. Take a holiday with your friends. *Meet people.* If you met someone you liked, you could, you know . . . have fun.

15

HAVE FUN. HIS words plague me. Every morning, on my way to school, I sit in a line of cars waiting to cross the bridge over the River Dodder. This is the bleakest hour, when dread rises and every moment feels precarious, and portents and premonitions have to be pushed down. In school, I move slowly, addressing every child and adult kindly and consciously, as if they too are hanging on a thread.

Peter does not bring up the subject again, and I grow a little hopeful that his proposition – his two propositions – were an aberration, a moment of madness. He is still grieving, I tell myself, he did not mean it. If I'm patient, if I do not fret or indulge my fears, this crisis will pass.

But I cannot bear the uncertainty, so just before he goes away to the Himalayas for the month of October, I bring it up.

—What you said that night, did you mean it?

He thinks for a moment, then sighs.

—Can we just leave it for now?

And I do, and I interpret this sigh and these words as another morsel of hope. This Himalayan trip will clear his mind. He will go to the top of the world and, from his high heaven, he will gaze upon the magnificent earth, and everything will be clarified and he will be renewed and filled with gratitude for the life he has.

In the days after his departure, I mentally track his flights, his arrival in Kathmandu, the journey out of the city, the trek to base camp. This is the longest period we'll be apart. Boo follows me everywhere. Every evening, after her walk, we stay home, counting time until Peter returns to us. At bedtime I lift her onto the bed, and she curls her body tight against mine for the night. At the weekend I spend hours gazing out at the garden, thinking, straining, finding fault with myself, racking my brain for the precise cause of Peter's discontent, and for what is exerting so much pressure on my mind.

I get a letter from Peter, posted from Kathmandu before they left for base camp — a light blue aerogramme letter like my grandmother used to send to America years ago. He tells me about the outbound flights, the city, the preparation and date of departure for the trek. *Look after yourself*, he says, and give my love to Boo.

I wake up from a disturbing dream one night. It is night-time and Peter is in his tent, high up in the Himalayas. He's in trouble — he's suffocating, unable to breathe. He is crying and calling out to me, *I should never have come.* The following night, another dream. Joan Long, a woman from his climbing club, walks into our living-room with a little boy of about two. The boy runs to Peter with his arms open wide, wanting to be lifted.

* * *

He is due home on October 28th. That evening, I prepare dinner and make an apple tart and set the table. His flight from London gets into Dublin at 5.15 p.m. Don't come to the airport, he'd said in the letter, I'll take a taxi. When he has not arrived by 8 p.m., I switch off the cooker. After the nine o'clock news I unset the table. Finally, just before 11 p.m., I hear a car pulling up outside, then his key in the door. In the hall, I open my arms to him, but his embrace is cold and lifeless, and I know instantly we are doomed.

He drops his rucksack and follows me into the kitchen and in those eight or ten steps the truth dawns on me: he has been with someone these past hours. We sit at the table, and he lifts Boo onto his lap and shows me photographs he had developed before he left Kathmandu. Jagged, snow-capped peaks. Blinding white snow. Clear blue sky. Peter in sunshades, smiling into the camera. Peter in full climbing gear — helmet, harness, crampons, an ice hammer in each hand — climbing vertically up a wall of ice.

I long to talk and touch him, but he will not meet my eye.

—I had a dream while you were away, I say, and I recount the dream in which he couldn't breathe. When I finish, he is staring at me.

—When was that, he asks, what date?

—Maybe a week or so after you left, I say. I wrote it down. I'll check it later.

He goes to the hall and gets his diary.

—I had one really bad night, he says, turning the pages. October 9th . . . It was after we got to base camp. We'd go to bed early every evening. It was very hard to sleep. The air is so thin at that altitude, it's hard to breathe. But that night it was really bad . . . I thought I was suffocating. I started to panic. I thought, what the hell am I doing here? . . . But I got through it. It was the only low point in the whole trip.

I know, without checking my dream journal, that the dates will match.

He looks at me, waiting for me to bring up the elephant in the room.

—What you said before, I say, do you still feel the same about us . . . about us ending?

He nods.

—Say it, I say.

—I still feel the same. I'm sorry.

I get up and drop a bunch of photographs on the table.

—Here, I say, I'm going to bed. You can sleep in the front room.

I pick Boo up in my arms and, as I turn to leave, I see the apple tart sitting on the hob, and the sight of it embarrasses me.

When I get in from school one afternoon, I sense something – a presence – in the living-room, as if someone has just been there. I stand in the middle of the room for a few moments and my eyes are drawn to the phone on the end table. I pick up the receiver and press the redial button. A man answers, says the name of a well-known hotel on the outskirts of the city. I hang up and scroll to the next number and hit redial again. A woman answers, Hello, and again, Hello, and when I say nothing, she is silent too. In the background there are children, a kitchen, a household. We both wait. Finally, she hangs up.

When Peter comes in, he has no explanation. He must have dialled a wrong number, he says.

Then, unexpectedly, the answer arrives one Saturday morning a few weeks later. We are having breakfast in a café in Rathmines.

—I never told you about the other dream I had while you were away, I say. In the dream, Joan Long – that woman who joined the climbing club last year – came into our living-room. She had a little boy with her, and the boy ran over to you and raised his arms to be picked up. He was about two.

Peter has turned white. He is staring at me as if I am a ghost.

—I was going to tell you, he says, almost whispering. I'm sorry. I was going to tell you.

It takes a moment for his words to register.

—What? . . . Joan Long. I say the name, barely comprehending.

He nods slowly. All the sounds of the café blend together in an indistinct hum.

—Joan Long? And you?

He nods. The café door opens and someone walks in and the door clicks closed again. I think if I get up and go to the bathroom, none of this will have happened when I return.

I remember the dream again. Is there a child?

He shakes his head. No . . . But she wants to have one for me. She's going to leave her husband too.

I keep looking at him as those words resound in my mind. I am trying to pull up words of my own. I look down into my coffee. What colour would you call coffee? I ask. Brown? No, toffee colour maybe.

—What?

—Her kids – remind me again, how old are they?

He shakes his head, but I push. How old?
—I'm not sure. Two and four maybe.
—She must be a wonderful mother.
—Stop.
—Was she in the Himalayas?
—No.
—Did she pick you up from the airport that night?
He nods.
—She sent us flowers when we lost the child last year, I say.
—She sent them from the climbing club, he says.
—How thoughtful, I say. She felt our pain.
—Stop, please.
—How old is she?
—Forty.

I'm thirty-one, I want to say. Then, because I'm afraid I'll be sick, I get up and walk carefully to the toilets at the back of the café. I sit in a cubicle for a long time. I understand now why my mind — my whole system — has been under duress. I met her once, briefly, when I dropped Peter to the start of a hike — a solid, big-boned woman, with a weatherbeaten, equine face. The word *Amazon* had crossed my mind at the time.

— You're such a coward, Peter, I say, when I return to the table. You hadn't the guts to tell me. I had to do it for you — I had to literally dream the truth.

The following Friday evening, I come home from school to find Peter's rucksack sitting in the hall, packed, but he is not there. Later, I lie on the bed with Boo beside me, the December light fading outside. As I'm drifting off to sleep, the phone rings. Boo lifts her head.

—Hi, is Peter there? a woman asks.
—No, I say.
—Okay, she says, thanks.

—I'm not gone yet, I tell him, when he comes in.
—I'm sorry about that, he says. It wasn't malicious, she didn't mean to –
—I'm your wife, Peter. It takes some gall to do that. The audacity! To call *my* home and ask for *my* husband. *My husband*. So desperate to get a hold of you – to find out if the weekend is on or off – that she doesn't put a tooth in calling your wife. That takes some neck.

But he is already on his feet, heading out the door.

The following Friday, the rucksack is packed and ready in the hall again.

—You can't keep doing this, I cry. You can't go off with her like this, and then come home to me. My chest is so tight I think it will crack open.

If I tell anyone – Elaine or my mother or Kathy – it will mean the end. Once people know, there is no going back, and I cannot be without him. I am not ready to give up. Couples get through affairs all the time. He has not committed a crime, he has not murdered anyone. Do I throw away eight years of marriage for an affair?

And then, just before Christmas, he comes in and sits across from me in the living-room, looking pale and shaken.

—I've ended it, he says. We're not going to see each other again.

16

HE WITHDRAWS DEEP into himself. His suffering is great, but I cannot help him, I cannot take it from him. I must be patient, ask no questions. But the days and weeks crawl by, and the doomed feeling never leaves.

Then, when spring arrives, he brightens. By early March he is back swimming. He spends four days climbing in Snowdonia and goes to Kerry for St Patrick's weekend. He has come through.

When he announces he's going to Scotland for Easter, my heart sinks.

—Peter, tell me if I'm rushing you, but we should be spending more time together . . . I don't think I'm being unreasonable, am I?

—You're not being unreasonable, he says.

—Is it too soon?

He shakes his head.

—You seem much better now, I say, and I thought things would have improved for us by now too. And I'm trying to be patient. I am! But I'm struggling . . . and I need to know certain things.

—What things?

—I need to know that you're committed to me, to us. We've been through a lot and . . . I don't know what else to do. I think we need help. I want us to go to counselling.

He shakes his head. Absolutely not! I'm not going to have a stranger tell me what to do.

—I don't have a good feeling, Peter, I say. You seem okay again – you're back living your life, like before. But I need to know that you're committed to me, to our marriage . . . What if we have kids? Will you be around? Will you be there for their birthdays and First Holy Communions and Confirmations or will you be away on the mountains? . . . I need to know. Will you commit to all that? Will you?

He shrugs and looks away.

—I don't know, he says. Then he looks directly at me. I've been seeing her again, he says.

—Kick him out, Elaine says. She is furious; she wants to fly home. He has to go. He's abusing you – and you're colluding with this. He was always a selfish asshole. I'm going to call him.

—Please, Elaine, stop, I say.

—What's wrong with you, Anna? Jesus Christ, he's walking all over you and you're letting him! This isn't normal. It's like you're missing the anger gene or something.

When he comes home on Sunday night, I tell him he has to go.

—You cannot have it both ways, I say.

A flash of anger then. Where will I go? This is my home too.

—I don't care where you go. You're not staying here.

The following Friday when I get home from school, I discover he's gone away with her again for the weekend. I want to howl or bang doors or break something, but I cannot frighten Boo. I go out and buy cigarettes. I have not smoked since college, so I inhale tentatively at first until my lungs are accustomed to the nicotine. After the first cigarette, I switch on the coffee machine and put coffee into the paper filter. The water gurgles and hisses and pale watery coffee dribbles through, then stops. The paper filter has collapsed and the coffee grounds have blocked the flow. I clear the mess, and refill the machine and start again. And again, the filter collapses and the coffee is ruined, and I break down. It is a sign, this minor domestic disruption is a sign, the last straw. I go upstairs, and pack a bag and put Boo into the car and drive west.

The light is fading when I arrive home. The signature tune of the nine o'clock news is playing when I walk into the kitchen. Alarmed at my sudden appearance, my mother tells my father to turn off the TV.

I tell them everything.

—I knew something was wrong, my mother says and she starts to cry.

My father gets up from his chair and puts his hand on my shoulder.

—You're doing the right thing, he says. Don't ever forget that.

Later that night I call Fintan, and then Elaine and I talk on the phone again for a long time.

*   *   *

When Peter gets home on Sunday night, he sniffs the air.

—Have you been smoking? he asks, annoyed.

I ignore him for a while.

—I've told my family, I say then. Everyone knows now.

He is thrown. He had not banked on my telling anyone. I am no longer the girl he married.

Now, the power has shifted. He seems less certain when he is in the house – he no longer answers the phone or the doorbell. On the day he is due to move out, his bags are in the hall when I arrive home from school, and he is sitting at the top of the stairs.

—Your father called this morning, he says.

—My father? Why?

—To berate me.

—How come you answered the phone?

—I was coming down the stairs when it started ringing and . . . I don't know – I just picked it up without thinking.

—What did you say to him?

—I didn't say anything, I just listened. He was raging . . . What sort of man are you, what kind of man would treat his wife this way? When I didn't answer he got more frustrated. He kept saying, Are you there? . . . He said he'd never trusted me, that there was something about me from the start that he never trusted.

—What else?

—He said you were a good wife. That you were too trusting . . . But mostly he gave out about me and my character.

I climb the stairs and sit beside him.

—I don't blame your father, he says. I'd probably do the same if I were in his shoes.

—You could never be in my father's shoes.

There is nothing else to say. It is time for him to leave. He has been in my life since I was nineteen years old.

—Can you love two people at the same time? he asks.

I do not reply, and we sit there for what seems a long time. He starts to cry.

—I think I've made the biggest mistake of my life, he whispers. You're the only person in the world I trust. I know I'll never be this loved again.

This is only the second time I have ever seen him cry.

I put my arm around his shoulder, but I feel nothing. These are crocodile tears — he is crying for himself, and for all he has lost.

17

HE CALLS ME from his new flat every night.

—I miss you, he says, his voice breaking. I cannot believe it has come to this.

He has no television and very little furniture. He is unaccustomed to solitude or discomfort. I have never known Peter to be ill, to have as much as a headache. He is without conflict, a man who is rarely, if ever, afflicted by his conscience. The self-pitying phone calls begin to wane after a week, and I know he is back to being himself again. In two months, when the tenants leave, he will move into his own house where he lived when we first met.

My mother calls every night too, asking how I am, and if I could take a few weeks off school and come home for a while. They are all worried about me. Fintan has started teaching in the university in Galway, and he wonders if I would consider moving west altogether. Elaine wants me to visit her in Brussels and when I decline, she offers to come to Dublin. All I want is to be alone, to lie on the couch with Boo every evening and think about Peter – where he is, who he's with, what he's doing.

When Boo lifts her head and looks at me, I am certain she understands. And then it hits me: what did she see? Was she privy to Peter's deception? Did he bring his woman to this house? When they went upstairs, did Boo seek out the furthest corner of the house – near the back door – from the sound of their exertions, and wait it out, her little heart racing, her little mind nervous and confused, worried that she was somehow party to this wrong?

Driving home from school one day, Fleetwood Mac's 'Songbird' comes on the radio, and I am blindsided by sorrow. I turn the car around and drive to Peter's flat complex, hoping to come upon him, longing to hear the voice that has lived in me all my adult life. Just to catch sight of him would be enough. I stop and let the engine idle and, in this strange lacuna of waiting and not waiting, it occurs to me that this was not his first affair, that he has always been unfaithful. Once, when we were in a café in the city centre, the door opened and two women walked in, and Peter, mid-sentence, slid down in his seat and pulled up the newspaper he'd been reading to hide his face. Another time, as we walked down Grafton Street, he ducked into a shop without warning. There were other duckings and divings, unexplained phone calls, sudden changes to work or travel schedules, moments when I did not heed my own intuition, when I brushed away nagging doubts. He had ample opportunity. I put the car in gear and accelerate away. What a fool I've been. But I, too, am to blame for not facing my fears, for not confronting him, for my own wilful blindness.

When the summer holidays arrive, I walk over to Xtra-vision every morning after breakfast and rent videos. I close the sitting-room curtains and, all day long, I watch movies back to back. *Taxi Driver, The Godfather, Mean Streets.* I can barely understand Robert De Niro's mumblings, but I cannot take my eyes off him. I turn the volume high in *The Deerhunter*. I rewind the scene where he is poised to shoot the deer. When the film ends, I rewind it and watch it all over again. I rent every De Niro film on Xtra-vision's shelves. *The Mission. Backdraft. Goodfellas. Midnight Run, A Bronx Tale, This Boy's Life.* I mouth his words. I wait for his smile, for the way he scrunches up his face and narrows his eyes when he smiles, and I do the same back at the screen. When De Niro puts his open mouth awkwardly, grotesquely, over Meryl Streep's in *Falling in Love,* I pause the video. I study his sighs – I believe they are real and he has fallen for Meryl in real life too. When the movie ends, the rattle of the Long Island Rail Road lingers in my ears for hours. But it is *Once Upon a Time in America,* more than any other film, that haunts me. I am hypnotised by Elizabeth McGovern's beautiful, startlingly white face, and by the terrible doomed chemistry between her character and De Niro's. When I climb the stairs to bed, the look in her pained eyes follows me.

Mornings are the most hopeful. On our walks, people stop to admire Boo and, briefly, I am back in the world again. At home, I settle down in front of the TV. By afternoon, if my stash of videos is running low, I suffer a mild panic before rushing over to Xtra-vision to replenish it. Some days, exhausted and defeated, I lie on the couch, faced inwards, obsessing about Peter, trawling over the past, until the light fades. Everything is turbulence now. Everything is gone, my life with Peter is gone. His family is gone from me too. Where once there was something, now there is nothing. One day I think: Was it all a sham, my life with Peter?

I concentrate hard, trying to pinpoint which part of it was not a sham. After the De Niro fixation, I move on to Pacino, then to Warren Beatty. I spend the summer in the darkened room, getting up only to feed and walk Boo and, occasionally, feed myself.

One Saturday late in August, I buy two CDs by Keith Jarrett in HMV. That night, I cook dinner and open a bottle of wine, and put on *The Köln Concert*. When Jarrett plays those opening notes and begins the climb in that first movement, I feel a faint stirring, a hint of hope. In the seventh minute, the notes trickle down before rising again and swelling into a gorgeous melody and I feel, for the first time in months, a flickering of joy.

Peter calls me one evening to say he's going to stop by. Finally, I think, I am able to face him, and reality. It is time to exchange solicitors' details. Although we cannot apply for a divorce until we've been living apart for four years, we can put a legal separation in place.

When he enters, he is tense and irritable. He stands in the middle of the room.

—This is unpleasant, he says. I wanted to tell you before I moved out. He pauses and sighs. You have to get yourself tested. Joan got chlamydia soon after we . . .

I stare at him, registering the word — its clotted sound, the incongruity of this word coming from his mouth into this room.

—It's a sexually transmitted disease, he says.

—I know what it is.

The word is ricocheting around my brain, and at the same time I am reaching back, trying to remember articles I've read in newspapers and magazines about sexually transmitted diseases, details about the damage they do.

—You need to get tested, he says. You might be fine, but you need to get tested.

—I might be fine?

—Look, I've told you . . . That's all I can do. I have to go now.

He bends down to pet Boo, but I snatch her up in my arms before he gets to her. Don't touch her, I say. He makes towards the door, but I block his way, flooded by thoughts and questions. And the dawning of a realisation.

—When did you get it? I ask.

—I don't know . . . I didn't know I had it until . . . Please, I have to go now.

—I was a virgin when we met, Peter. You know that. You know that I've never slept with anyone else.

He nods.

—At the start, when I had trouble getting pregnant, Dr Boland asked me about my sexual history. Did he ask you about yours?

He looks at the ground, shakes his head. I don't remember.

—I bet you infected me, I say. I bet you gave me chlamydia . . . and that's what caused all my problems.

—We don't know that.

I shake my head slowly. I *always* felt something was wrong, I say. Deep down, there was always some . . . fear gnawing at me. You were never faithful, were you, Peter?

Then a thought strikes me.

—Did you visit prostitutes? Did you sleep with men, Peter?

—No, Anna, I never slept with men, or visited prostitutes.

—I don't believe a word you say any more.

—So why ask me? I have to go now.

—Are you still seeing her?

—I don't want to talk about that . . . That was a mistake.

—So, Amazon woman isn't the love of your life after all, I say, with a sarcastic little laugh. Now, if only I hadn't had the bad luck to dream that dream and uncover your deceit, we might still be married, and I'd be none the wiser! I'd still be lying awake at night, trying to fathom what was wrong with us — blaming myself for being needy — while you were out whoring around.

I step out of his way, but he does not move.

—How did she know she had it? I ask.

—She had symptoms.

I turn away, crushed. I remember the bleeding, the pain, in the weeks and months after I first slept with him.

—There's a walk-in clinic in St James's, he says, if you . . .

I walk to the hall and open the front door.

—Get out, I say.

18

I TEST POSITIVE for chlamydia, negative for everything else. My voice is breaking when I ask the consultant if this could have been the cause of my fertility difficulties.

—Sadly, yes, she says. Chlamydia, if left untreated, wreaks havoc on a woman's reproductive organs. It's a serious bacterial infection that damages and blocks the fallopian tubes, and even if the tubes are unblocked later, a woman can suffer ectopic pregnancies. So, yes, in your case – from everything you've told me – I don't doubt that this is what happened.

She assures me that once I've completed the course of antibiotics she has prescribed, I will be completely free of infection.

—You have conceived before, she says, so there is no reason to believe you won't conceive again, and go full term.

I have, unknowingly, ferried this disease around in my body for years. I am sullied, tarnished, irrevocably damaged. This is the mark Peter has left on me – this is his legacy. The scarring will remain forever, until my flesh turns to dust or ashes. Images of the bacteria and the chain of transmission besiege my mind, with Peter, like a slithering worm, moving darkly from link to link. The pixie girl, the officer on the oil tanker, the Amazon woman – these I can identify. But it is the random women picked up in cafés or swimming pools, on climbing trips or sea voyages, the one-night stands and short flings and long affairs – hundreds, maybe – that are impossible to compute. How many of them – of *us*, because I must now count myself one of this sexual cohort – are riddled with disease? I am so full of shame that I will never speak about this. It is a secret I will keep for life.

As if provenance has decreed it, I come upon prostitutes everywhere – in novels and biographies and films. Did Graham Greene, who kept a list of forty-seven prostitutes with whom he had sex, or Georges Simenon, who boasted of having slept with ten thousand women, most of them prostitutes, ever consider the lives of these women and girls? Did Joyce, who visited prostitutes from the age of fourteen and ridiculed them in *Ulysses*, give thought to the destitute women on the back streets of Dublin, many of whom were country girls lured into prostitution on arrival in the city? I read everything I can find on Monto, the red-light district of Dublin's inner city in the early twentieth century, and become obsessed with these women's lives; the madams who pimped them at varying levels of service, from well-groomed girls in the grander establishments who ministered to the sexual pangs of royals, politicians and wealthy businessmen . . . all the way down to the miserable, wretched girls who serviced soldiers and paupers in the alleyways for a penny a go or a bottle of beer. All the unseen suffering they endured – syphilis, gonorrhoea, the pain of childbirth and urinary tract infections – and still they had to lie down and have their bodies pummelled, just to survive. How could Joyce – who had a kind heart, who had a wife and daughter and sisters he loved – ridicule these women, even in fiction, belittle them with his Biddy the Clap and Cunty Kate? And Peter. Was Peter ever haunted by the face of that poor Arab child who was offered to him in the hovel in Yemen? He refused the offer, he said, but how do I know? In a second-hand bookshop, one day, I come across a memoir by André Gide. *If It Die*. Camus admired Gide for his sensitive soul, so I buy the book. Gide describes his trips to North Africa, his nights out in Algiers with Oscar Wilde and Lord Alfred Douglas. He writes of the sensual pleasures he enjoyed in taking young Arab boys into his bed. I read the same paragraph over and over. The language is lyrical. The physical act that Gide calls *tender* and *achingly beautiful* is rape, the brutal penetration of these bare-foot, impoverished little boys.

Peter and I communicate only through our solicitors now. I want nothing more to do with him, but my psyche refuses to shed him. I see him on the street in Terenure sometimes. Last week I caught sight of him entering the bank and, for a second, I thought, *there's Peter*, and I almost blew the horn, like I'd do in the old days. I drive around nervously, defensively, now, expecting to see him. I spotted him sitting outside Café Java on South Anne Street with a young woman one Saturday, and I knew that if they were not already lovers, they soon would be. A conjugal couple, an intimate pair. He is almost fifty, and I no longer belong to him. I no longer know what he thinks, or how his days unfold, and I wish I did not care. At night, I think: Why did I stay with him so long? If I had left, who would have protected me, who would I have belonged to? How much of the marriage was a lie? It would help, I tell myself, if I could calculate the proportion of our life together that was *not* a lie, if I could wind back the years, track back through every day and hour and minute and find the laughter, the love, those surges when I *know* our thoughts streamed across to each other, and if, on finding them, there was a way to decipher and measure every facet of feeling in each of us — a scientific method or instrument, a *feelings* spectrometer — and if every feeling tone, from the terrible and the dim to the glorious and the radiant, could be logged and converted into neurological data — a kind of neuro-text that could be used in a mathematical formula or equation — then it might be possible to calculate the precise truth-to-lies ratio of our life together. And then I would know. Then I would know. But this result, too, would be flawed, because the ratio of truth would be elevated by *my* portion of the feeling data because did I not love him more? Still, it would be something, it would be some kind of measure of *us*. I could at least tell myself, Well, our marriage had a truth quotient of sixty-eight per cent, or, Our life together was seventy-four per cent truthful.

Mark, his brother, calls me.
　—What happened? he asks. The whole family is in shock.
　—Talk to Peter, I say.
　—He won't tell us anything. He says only that you've separated. My mother is devastated — she's very fond of you. Please, Anna, tell me.
　—He had an affair. I don't think it was his first.

After six months, we sign a Separation Agreement which will suffice until we can commence divorce proceedings. Immediately, I set about clearing out the house. In the attic, I come upon some letters I wrote to Peter throughout the marriage, but never gave him — long, heartfelt notes of hurt and upset, grievances I have long forgotten. I sit on the attic floor and read.

Why do you always put me down? Why are you so cruel, so mean? . . .

This is the second Christmas I have to go to Galway alone . . .

I'm sorry, you're right, I AM too needy, too bound up with my family. I need to separate from them . . .

You only ever do what you want. Sometimes I think you don't even like being married . . .

Please, Peter, come to Kathy's wedding, I beg you, I can't go alone . . .

I hate the thought of that crèche. I cannot bear the thought of leaving our baby with total strangers . . .

Today, I sat in the dining-room for hours mulling over everything. Please Peter, tell me what's wrong with us?

This is torment. Do you think I'm made of stone?

One afternoon, I am sitting in the dentist's chair, about to have a cavity filled. Ciarán, the dentist, is handsome, kind, gentle. There are photographs of his children on the wall. He tries to put me at ease, then works in my mouth, pausing now and then to ask if I'm okay. I nod, but I am tense, waiting for the drill. When the whirring begins, I close my eyes, my whole body taut and primed for the excruciating pain when the drill hits a nerve. When it stops, he asks again if I'm okay. The tenderness in his voice reminds me of Dr Boland. His fingers work inside my mouth, and as he strains and flexes to pack the tooth cavity, he leans against me, oblivious, for a moment, that my head is pressed against his chest, my face against his white coat, so that I can hear the thump of his heart. It has been such a long time since I've been physically close to a man that tears well up and when the first one slides off my face onto the black leather chair, I know I must change my life.

Within a few months, I take up a new school position closer to the city. I'm no longer teaching in a regular class, but working with troubled children, children with social and emotional difficulties. I put the house on the market and, as soon as it sells, I buy an old redbrick house overlooking a small park, within walking distance of my new school. Boo cannot believe her luck – three times a day, she trots around the park, revelling in her new kingdom. I let her off the lead and she runs up to children and chases other dogs, and I smile at her good fortune.

I am thirty-two, and it seems like I have lived the greater portion of my life, and now I am ready to withdraw from the world.

Part 2

19

THE BAR IS called Samsara, a series of long rooms with high ceilings and marble pillars that run deep into an elegant Georgian building on Dawson Street. Mirrors on the walls, mosaic tiles on the floor, giant potted plants in corners. On the sound system, Shakira is singing, then Alicia Keyes. I am with Sinéad, a friend from school, who has been nudging me out into the world again. It has been almost five years since Peter and I parted, and a year since I instructed my solicitor to set in motion my application for a divorce. Put the past behind you, Sinéad said, get out and meet people.

The bar is crowded and I am lightheaded from the wine and the music. Mary J. Blige, Destiny's Child. I spot him first, standing at the counter three or four metres away, with another guy. Two dark-skinned men in a bar full of white people. When our eyes meet, he smiles. Nelly Furtado is playing. I'm like a bird. He offers me a cigarette and I accept.

—Here we are, I say, in this endless, banal cycle of life and death and rebirth.

He smiles, confused, and I regret my attempt at cleverness.

—I'm never sure, I say, whether Samsara is something Buddhists must escape from or try to resist. But either option can't be right, can it, if non-resistance is the central tenet of Buddhism? I should stop, I'm even making myself nervous now.

His name is Karim and he is French. He and his friend, Mateo, are software engineers with Intel. Karim lives astonishingly close to me – in an apartment block overlooking the canal. We might have passed each other in the park, I say. After a few minutes of conversation, he stops suddenly.

—I'm Algerian actually, not French, he says, nervously. I was born in Algiers, I just went to school in France.

—Oh, I say. Algiers. Images of Camus, and Camus's mute mother, and the city's sun and sky and sea come unbidden.

—Do you know Algiers? he asks.

I shake my head. Do you know Albert Camus? I ask.

—Ah, the writer. He was a goalie for a soccer team in Algiers.

—Yes! Do you know his books?

He shakes his head. I'm sorry, I'm afraid it's mostly code I read.

Sinéad is talking to Mateo. She is engaged to be married, and was ready to leave half an hour ago, but she is one of the kindest people I know. She minds Boo whenever I have to go to a family wedding or a funeral down the country.

When we are about to leave, Karim asks for my number.

I give him a look of mock appalment. Why would I give you my number? I tease.

I am thirty-seven, but tonight, with the wine and the music and this otherworldly bar, I feel young and free and daring, a different self. Karim's foreignness, too, frees me. Earlier, when an Irish man tried to chat me up, I frowned and barely answered, giving off an air of haughtiness that belied the terror and the urge to flee I felt.

When Karim asks again, I smile and rhyme off my mobile number at speed.

—Ah, not fair, he laughs.

—You're an engineer, I say, you must be good with numbers . . . Okay, last chance . . .

He holds up a finger. One second, please. He leans over to Mateo and gets a pen. Dido is singing.

—Okay, he says, go.

The following Sunday, my doorbell rings. When I open the door Boo runs out and startles Karim. He is holding out a pack of ten Silk Cut Blue cigarettes.

—For you, he says. He was passing my house on his way home from Centra. He has a beautiful smile.

As he stands, framed in the open door, backlit by the sunlight and the huge old trees of the park, I have an overwhelming sense of déjà vu. I say something – hello, maybe. I am transfixed, arrested by a memory and a realisation. Two years ago, not long after I moved in here, Karim announced himself in a dream, and now that dream floods my mind. It was summer, and I was in the park with fellow students from my university days, lying there, chatting, languishing in the sun. Then William, our psychology professor, came out of my house, down the steps and crossed to the park with an urgent message for me. Ahmad phoned, he said, asking to speak to you. I don't know any Ahmad, I said. But William was emphatic. You must call him immediately, he said. It is imperative that you speak to him. Go, the others urged, you have to go! And it dawned on me — on my dream self — that I had no choice, that this call with Ahmad was vital, momentous. When I stood up, they all began to congratulate me, as if I was about to be married. I walked towards the house, my heart full of joy and expectation and, as I moved, I could see clearly — on the edge of my consciousness — a beautiful, framed page of text in a script I could not read. The page was surrounded by a decorative border in red and blue patterns. And there the dream ended. But it took hold and remained with me for a long time, one of those powerfully numinous dreams that I knew from my Jungian study was significant, but whose meaning I could not fathom then.

Karim is still holding out his gift, and I stare at it, as if it is something I have never seen before. Then, surprised by the lightness of the cigarette pack, I smile and say, Thank you. I invite him in, but he declines. Boo is sniffing his shoes, and he is watching her and discreetly trying to withdraw each foot from her reach. When I close the door, I am shaken — not so much by Karim's visit as by the dream visitation. Is Karim Ahmad? Did my unconscious anticipate Karim two years ago? How is that possible?

All evening long, I cannot put this dream coincidence, this serendipity, out of my mind. When night falls, I consult the I Ching. I have made a habit of consulting it at times of doubt or uncertainty. It is how I live now — wary of fate, fearful of chance. I want to ascertain Karim's significance and decide if I should see him again. The reading does not augur well. The hexagram's commentary indicates that retreat is the best path.

But the dream seemed portentous, and I am drawn to Karim, and so, defying the age-old injunction not to consult the I Ching on the same issue twice, I throw the coins again the next day. Again, the hexagram's counsel is to retreat. At crucial times, we see what we want to see, and hear what we want to hear, and I convince myself that there is enough ambiguity in the commentary's archaic language to allow for a positive interpretation. So, with uncharacteristic recklessness, I defy the oracle and tempt fate, and as I skip into the city to meet Karim on Friday evening, I have the sense that I am leaving one stream of life and entering another.

20

KARIM DJEBAR IS thirty-four. He has lived in Dublin for almost five years. Before that, he spent four years in London, where his sister Nadia lives with her husband and daughter.

He stops by regularly with cigarettes and little treats – a bar of chocolate, a blueberry muffin.

—I was just passing, he says.

He has a courteous manner, an old-fashioned chivalry that reminds me of my father and his generation of men. He meets me at the school gates one afternoon on a day off work, and walks me home through the park. On Friday evening he plays soccer with his workmates, and afterwards comes over for dinner. At the sight of him on my doorstep, my heart leaps. He has a boyishness – a shy smile and an uncertain demeanour – that, after years of Peter's authoritative manner, surprises and delights me.

He asks about my vegetarianism, and when I tell him I cannot bear to eat animals, he is baffled.

—But you grew up on a farm and you give meat to your dog! he says.

Boo lifts her head from her bed. He never says her name or gives her any attention.

—She's very gentle, I say. You don't have to be nervous of her.

—It's not that . . . He smiles at Boo.

—Do you not like dogs? I ask.

—I'm more of a cat person, he says.

—Oh, I say, suddenly remembering a scene in a movie once, where a Muslim man crossed the street to avoid a dog, Is it because you're Muslim?

He nods. Muslims believe that angels won't enter a house where there's a dog, he says.

—Cover your ears, Boo, I say, and he laughs. I want to ask if he believes that too.

After dinner we walk to the pub up the road.

—You have beautiful eyes, he says. I am sitting on a high stool at the bar. I cannot recall a single occasion when Peter complimented me.

—That night we met, I say, you said you were French, before you corrected yourself. Why did you say that? You're fully Algerian – you just went to school in France.

—I'm sorry . . . He looks at me. It's not easy being a Muslim this past year, since September 11th. People are suspicious. I was being cautious.

I know no other Muslims. Occasionally, on the streets, I see African women and Asian and Middle-Eastern students in headscarves but, over my lifetime, I have rarely encountered Muslims, and my impression of them has derived, mostly, from TV images. Stampedes at the annual Hajj in Mecca. Yasser Arafat in fatigues and a keffiyeh. Suicide bombings in Israel.

Chaotic funerals in the West Bank — open coffins above jostling crowds, women in black wailing in grief. Or, more recently, Afghani women in blue burqas. F-16s raining down bombs on Gaza. Over the years, news reports of violence in the Middle East competing with news reports of violence in Northern Ireland, and images, names and places eliciting the same sense of ennui. Now, sitting here with Karim, I am ashamed of my ignorance, and respond only with silence.

I am enchanted by the stories of his family and his childhood. His father was a civil engineer in the transport department in Algiers until, eventually — when he could no longer turn a blind eye to the corruption — he was fired.

—It's still a corrupt regime, Karim says. They're all corrupt — the generals, the civil servants . . . No one is honest. My father opened a little newsagent's downtown then. They did everything to try and shut him down, but . . . Masha'Allah, people liked my father, and they kept coming back . . . I was a child then, he says. I used to bring the poorer boys there on our way home from school and order my father — Give him sweets, I'd say. Give him pastries!

We are in Karim's apartment. I am curled up on his couch, lulled and seduced by his voice and the world he is describing. And by his goodness, his innocence and sincerity.

—My father's father came to the city from the countryside — from the Kabyle, he says. They kept goats on the mountainside and lived simple lives. My father took me there when I was a boy. Tizi Ouzou. It's very beautiful. Hills covered in wildflowers overlooking the sea. Completely silent at night, with just the stars. He smiles. I will take you there some day.

As he speaks, Camus flashes through my mind. Camus among the ruins at Tipasa, with the warm stones and the rhythm of light and heat, and the kissing sound of the sea. Or at Djémila where his soul was washed by the wind and the sad song of death. Beauty and sorrow combined. How is it that, whenever I think of Camus, my soul is moved to tears?

—My grandfather had no education, Karim is saying. He worked menial jobs. But he made sure my father was educated. Here, he says, holding out some photographs, this is my father at home in our house.

His father is elderly, slight, with small smiling eyes. He's wearing a little round hat, the kind I've seen Muslim men wear on their way to the mosque on South Circular Road on Fridays. He's sitting in a large room with heavy dark furniture and behind him, there's a terrace or courtyard with a view out over rooftops and trees and, in the distance, the hazy sea. I have the impression of a villa in a nice residential neighbourhood above Algiers, somewhere like Parc d'Hydra where Camus lived during his brief, disastrous marriage to Simone Hié.

—Who's this? I ask, picking up a photograph of a young boy in a soccer shirt, holding a football.

Karim beams a big smile. This is Youssef, my nephew, my eldest sister's boy in Algiers.

—He's very cute. How old is he?

—Eleven, soon twelve. He is a beautiful boy . . . very sweet, and obedient to his parents, and to his sister. The best son a mother could ask for. Then he gives a little laugh. He is like a son to me too! I bought him his first bike and taught him to cycle. My sister and her husband are not well off. He keeps gazing at Youssef's picture. I will bring him here to go to university, he says.

He shows me more photographs, all the family around a table.

—Are they religious, your parents? I ask.

He makes a so-so gesture with his hand.

—They fast for Ramadan, he says, and they give Zakat — alms. My father goes to Friday prayer. They don't drink, or eat pork . . . They are normal, like most Muslims. He looks at me, a flicker of anger or defiance in his eyes. We're not terrorists, he says.

—I never thought you were.

21

I TELL NO one about Karim in the beginning. Sinéad, who has just moved into a beautiful house in Ranelagh, invites me to a dinner party. There are eight of us, all women. Séamus, her husband, helps to serve and then goes off to watch TV. The food is delicious. The conversation is mostly about property prices, cars, private schools. Sinéad's sister has recently returned from living in Saudi Arabia with her engineer husband. Suddenly they are talking about Muslims.

—The wealth is staggering, she says. The women can have all they want, materially, but they have no real rights. I saw it at first-hand – how the men control them. They cannot even drive a car, and they just accept it.

—I can't *stand* Muslims, a woman at the far end of the table says. Look at the Middle East – the attacks on Israel. They don't want peace.

Others join in, spew out words. Al-Qaeda. Jihadists. Suicide bombers. My heart is racing. I try to summon up the courage to speak, to tell them the truth, but I am paralysed.

—When I was a teenager, another woman says, a girl in

our school used to warn us. Don't ever marry a Muslim, she'd say. They'll steal your babies and take them away. And she wasn't far wrong.

Later, I walk out into the night, dazed. I realise that no woman I know — not Sinéad, or Sinéad's sister, or my own sister or the girls I knew in college — has ever gone out with a Muslim, and probably never would.

Karim cooks dinner at his flat one evening, a vegetarian dish with sweet peppers and courgettes. I can taste chicken — he has used chicken stock. I swallow hard and pick out the vegetables and say nothing. I cannot bear to hurt him. On Al Jazeera, there's a report from the West Bank on the demolition of Palestinian homes to make way for an illegal Israeli settlement. We watch in silence as Palestinians attempt to block a bulldozer before it ploughs through the crowd and flattens a house. Women and children flee with whatever belongings they can save. A little girl of about five or six runs from the wreckage, carrying a plastic basin with a few cups and plates. Karim leaves down his plate, unable to eat. Without a word, he gets up and goes to the bathroom and, while he is gone, I switch channels.

On Sunday, he dials up the internet and, on a map of Algiers, points to the street in the hills above the city where his parents live, then shows me where his sister lives, and where his father's shop was located.

—Show me your school, I say, and the mosque your father goes to. And the Kasbah. I tell him that Camus lived in Belcourt. Most of the street names have reverted to Arabic now. Rue de Lyon, where Camus lived in a small apartment with his mother, brother, grandmother and uncle, is now named rue Mohamed Belouizdad.

In the afternoon, we cross the city to the Botanic Gardens and walk along the paths, under trees. In the silence and yearning between us, I have a glimpse, a brief flicker, of future possibilities.

Karim takes my hand and sighs. Ah, Anna Marie Hughes, what are you doing to me? he says quietly.

We sit on a bench. Already, I know — I can feel it — what Karim is bestowing on me: love, tenderness, truth. But I know, too, how dangerous it is to let him — or anyone — into my solitary life, into my loneliness, because some day he will leave.

—You don't see your family very often, do you? I ask. Don't you miss them?

He laughs. Are you trying to get rid of me already?

—Far from it. But I sense you're close to them.

—I do miss them. Every day. And my parents are getting old. I feel guilty I'm not there for them. But I don't miss the culture, the corruption, the society. Algeria is like most of the Middle-Eastern and Arab regimes — they're all the same. They give Muslims a bad name. I get angry with the media in the West for how we're portrayed, but it's as much the fault of Muslim leaders. You know who is the worst culprit? Saudi Arabia, the cradle of Islam. The sheiks, the ministers, they are all liars, thieves, tyrants. They're not real Muslims! I exclude the citizens, the ordinary people — I don't fault them.

I am taken aback by his outburst.

—Do you know the most Islamic country on earth? he asks, softly, after a few moments.

I shake my head.

—Ireland, he says. In the way it treats people, it is truly

Islamic. The UK is okay, too, but here the state looks after the poor, the sick, the disabled — you look after immigrants. And the way this country cares for the elderly — you give them a pension and free medical care and free travel — is like nowhere else on earth. That's the biggest sign of a caring society.

—You're welcome! I say, relieved, puffing out my chest.

—I'm sorry for the rant. I get frustrated — the damage these Arab regimes do to the perception of Islam! I have five sisters; they all went to university — two are teachers. My oldest sister is a professor of comparative religions in the University of Algiers. In Islam girls and women *must* be educated. Mohammed's wife Khadija was a successful businesswoman! People in the West don't know this — they are so . . .

—Ignorant?

He laughs. Uninformed, he says.

—Tell me about Islam, I say, later, over coffee.

—What do you want to know? he asks cautiously.

—Anything. Everything. The thing is, I don't know if there is a God.

—Ah, but you don't know that there isn't! he shoots back, with a wry smile.

—True. I used to be quite religious when I was young.

—So . . . then there is hope.

—For me?

—Yes.

—But you're not a practising Muslim, Karim, are you? You drink . . . Do you pray?

His face darkens. I'm not a good Muslim, Anna, he says. I am ashamed. Maybe one day we will both return to God.

I laugh. Are you trying to convert me?

—You don't need to convert. You were born Muslim – everyone is. You'd just be reverting to your original faith. Anyway, there's no compulsion in Islam. He is smiling, like a parent teasing a child to do their bidding.

—Reverting . . . Mmm, I'm not sure how that would go down with my folks.

He looks out the window.

—Everything – all of nature – is Muslim, he says. Look, even the trees out there are bowing down to Allah. That's what Zahra, my grandmother, used to say. She knew the names of all the flowers and grasses – they are all bequeathed by Allah, she'd say. She came to live with us in the city. She was terrified of the traffic and the blaring horns. I used to hear her crying at night. She thought we were uncivilised! I think she found it hard to find Allah in the city. My father took her back to the Kabyle for burial.

I tell him about my own grandmother.

—I used to go to daily Mass with her in the summer, I say. I was a prayerful child. The world was different then.

I remember those mornings. We walked in silence, past wildflowers in the ditch and little birds in the hedgerow. I could feel the beating heart of all that existed in that hedgerow. In those lit-up moments, I was exalted. I knew the meaning of God's grandeur long before I heard of Gerard Manley Hopkins. But, as I got older, I grew cautious and fearful. By age twelve, I would run past the church on dark evenings, intoning a prayer, *Sacred heart of Jesus, I place all my trust in thee*, terrified that the Blessed Virgin would appear and speak to me and mark me out for life with some revelation.

22

WHEN KARIM STAYS overnight for the first time, I tell him that Peter was my first and only lover.

—I'm embarrassed, I say, telling you this.

He frowns and shakes his head. I cannot tell if he is nonplussed by my embarrassment or by the fact that, in this day and age, a single woman of my age has only had one lover. He asks no questions. He is, at first, reluctant to tell me about his own past. He was in a relationship with an English woman in London for a few years, and before that he lived, for a short time, with a Swedish woman in Paris. I ask for details, names, dates, durations, and he laughs, tells me I'm a strange woman. We talk for hours and drift off to sleep, and then wake and talk some more and finally, in the morning, we make love.

We stay in bed for hours, talking and making love. He makes love slowly, generously – an unselfish lover.

I am lying with my head on his stomach. He has a small scar on his left side. When I touch it, he removes my hand and kisses it tenderly.

—What is it? I whisper, but he does not answer.

Later, he shows me a photograph, taken when he was sixteen. He is so gaunt and emaciated that I would not have recognised him.

—My parents sent me to Paris to live with my older brother so I could go to a good school. I was very homesick. Rachid was good to me, but his wife . . . not so much. I helped her with the kids and everything. She gave me different food to the rest of the family. He chuckles. I wasn't allowed to eat their jam. Rachid was always at work, so he didn't know. He smiles. She just didn't want me there, I think.

I can picture him, a meek and willing boy, far from home, helping with housework, shopping, minding the kids.

—I hated Paris, but I wanted to study medicine. I worked very hard in school, year after year, preparing for the Baccalaureate. I had to get up in the dark and take a long bus journey and then get the Métro to the lycée – which was far away. I remember being weak and exhausted for a long time, but I thought it was normal, so I told no one. And I was very lonely, I missed my mother . . . I missed Algiers too, the sun and the beaches and the people. One morning on the way to school, I collapsed on the Métro and was taken to hospital, unconscious. They did lots of tests, but they didn't know what was wrong. It was touch and go for a while – I was close to death. I don't remember much from those first days. I woke one day, and my mother was there . . . She came from Algiers and sat by my bedside for months.

Finally, Karim tells me, he was diagnosed with inflammation of the digestive tract, a condition that was triggered by stress and anxiety. He had surgery and, altogether, spent two months in hospital.

—I was on steroids which made me very hungry, he says, laughing. There was an old man in the next bed and I was so hungry that I used to get up in the night and take food from his locker. He shakes his head. It was very hard. The old man eventually died – that was very frightening. Anyway, I missed out on the Baccalaureate that year, and by the time I got back to school, my friends had all gone on to university. And after that, I was in and out of hospital a bit and, I don't know . . .

I stare at the photograph of the gaunt teenage boy, and my heart is full of love and pity for him and for the man before me now who brings me little gifts and believes in God and says Insha'Allah at every turn.

On Saturday morning we take the bus into the city. I feel strange, self-conscious, walking down Grafton Street with a man who is not Peter, as if I expect to be stopped and questioned. *Who is this man, this foreign man, who is not your husband?* Karim buys jeans and t-shirts and football boots to send to Youssef for his birthday. In Hodges Figgis I buy a biography of Mohammed by Karen Armstrong.

We stop at a flower-seller. Karim wants to buy me lilies, but I shake my head and point to our shopping bags. Another time, I say. We turn onto South Anne Street and, as if primed, my eyes find Peter sitting outside Café Java, his usual haunt. He is with a woman, again, but it is not Amazon woman, nor is it, as far as I tell, the young woman he was with previously. I am about to turn back to Grafton Street, but he has seen me, and our eyes meet. He scans me and then scans Karim and when his eyes meet mine again, he has a smirk on his face, a mocking look. A familiar sense of shame and foreboding envelops me, as if Peter still has authority over me, as if I am still answerable to him.

—We just passed my husband, I say, when we turn onto Dawson Street.

Karim's eyes widen. He stops and swings around. Where? Where is he? he asks.

I have not told Karim everything about the marriage, but enough that each time I told him something new, I saw pain in his eyes. You have no firewall, Anna, he told me once.

—He's back there, with a woman.

—Let's go back. I want to see this . . . bastard.

—No! Are you crazy? Keep walking. I smile and take Karim's hand. He has never used bad language before.

In Lemon Café, he queues at the counter for coffee and, when I'm seated, he winks and gives me a high beckoning nod, and I feel his protection.

—I want to see him, he says, when we finish the coffee. Let's go back, he might still be there.

—Absolutely not. I don't trust you – you'd probably confront him.

—I would. He's a jerk, Anna, the way he treated you.

—That's all in the past. Peter is just a man outside a café now.

But I feel an old, familiar pall descending. Will my eyes always seek him out in the crowd in this city? Will the sight of him always rattle me? Will I never be free of Peter?

23

I BRING KARIM west to meet my family. Elaine and her husband, Alain, are home on holidays and Fintan is there for the weekend too. He is thirty-three now, and has recently moved in with his beautiful lawyer girlfriend, Madeleine.

Gorgeous, Elaine mouths, behind Karim's back after we arrive. Later, my mother tells me he looks like a young Omar Sharif. He addresses her as Mrs Hughes. She is warm and at ease with him, asking him about his own parents, about Algeria. Mr Hughes, on the other hand, is quiet and circumspect. He is watching Karim, sizing him up as I imagine he once sized Peter up. My father is almost seventy now and has lost some vitality, and grown sombre. He would have liked Fintan to take over the running of the farm, but that is unlikely now. After dinner, Fintan takes Karim for a walk around the farm. Afterwards I can tell he likes Karim.

—He's out there now, the poor guy, having a smoke, he says. I think he's lost weight after the ordeal of meeting the whole family.

* * *

Back in Dublin on Monday, Karim does not respond to my texts and calls. By bedtime I begin to worry. There are moments when I sense uncertainty in him, when I think he has doubts about us, about our relationship. But I realise I hardly know him — there is something about him that resists being known. After school on Tuesday I walk down by the canal to his apartment complex. His car space is empty. I check again late in the evening, and his car is there, so I assume he has been to work. When I try calling him, his phone goes straight to messages. I enter the apartment complex and press his bell. A woman's voice answers. Hello. I freeze and say nothing. Suddenly the door buzzes and clicks open, and I am in the front hall. He is with a woman, I know he is with a woman. I run up the stairs in a blind panic, and stand outside his door, trying to listen against the terrible pounding in my chest. Silence. They are inside the door, I am certain, Karim holding a finger to his lips. I knock harder this time, and then run up the half flight of stairs to the quarter landing where I can hide and still have a view of his door. After a few moments, the door opens, and Karim puts his head out and looks down the stairwell. When he goes inside, I run down and knock again.

—Anna? What are you doing here? He looks sleepy and dishevelled.

—You have someone there. You have a woman inside.

He makes a face. I have no woman inside, he says.

—Can I come in?

—Now is not a good time. I don't feel well. I'm sorry . . .

I can smell alcohol on his breath. You're lying, I say. I rang your bell — a woman answered.

He shakes his head. That's not possible. There's no woman. I'm alone. He stands back. Come in and see for yourself.

I race around his apartment, frantically checking the wardrobe, behind doors, under the bed. His bed is unmade, and the lamp is on.

—I rang your bell, I say. I rang number thirty-six. *I did.*

—Maybe you pressed the wrong one . . . It's okay, it's a simple mistake. There's no harm done.

I shake my head. I rang your bell, I know I did. You think I'm crazy, don't you? I'm not crazy.

—I don't think you're crazy. It's just a mistake, a misunderstanding.

His eyes are soft, full of compassion, and I start to cry. He comes and puts his arms around me.

—Have you been drinking? I ask, suspicious again.

He nods.

I pull away. You did have someone here, didn't you? How did she leave? I look around, at the window, the door. I feel nauseous. I'm being fooled. It is like before, with Peter.

—Please stop. There's no one here. I was in the pub – in The Stone Boat. Alone. He looks down and shakes his head. I'm no good, Anna. I'm a Muslim, I shouldn't be drinking.

I sit on the side of the bed. What's wrong, Karim? Why are you drinking . . . alone, on a Tuesday evening?

He turns away, puts his head in his hands.

—Please, tell me, what's wrong? Are you ill? . . . Is it us? Is it something I did?

—It's not you, it's not us. He sits on the couch and stares at the floor. I got bad news yesterday, he says, about Youssef.

—Youssef? Your nephew?

He nods. He's dead.

The child had gone down to buy a Coke in the corner shop. When he came out of the shop, he walked straight into a shoot-out between the army and anti-government militants, and was caught in the crossfire.

—When? When did this happen?

—Last week. They never told me. My father called me yesterday . . . Maybe they thought they were sparing me, they knew I'd be upset. He's already buried. I don't blame them, they're devastated, they're all in shock.

Before Youssef's mother got down to the street, his body had already been picked up and taken to a military hospital on the other side of the city.

—They just threw his little body onto the back of an army truck, he says, like a sack of potatoes. My sister and her husband went to the military hospital to reclaim their son, but the gates were locked. They were told nothing. Every morning, they went to the gates, begging for their son's body. Can you imagine? Can you imagine their desperation?

I stand and put my arms around him, but he pulls away.

—Beautiful, innocent Youssef . . . You know whenever I gave him sweets, he would always put two aside. These are for Allah, he'd say.

He starts to pace the floor.

—Barbarians, that is what they are. Tyrants! I hate my country! Three days Maryam and Samir were left standing at the gates, begging for their son, before they got him back . . .

Later, in the bathroom, I find a notebook, open, and a pen resting on the edge of the bath. A line divides a page vertically.

Good job	34 years old
No debt	Smoking
Car	Drinking
	Sex
	Not praying
	Not fasting
	No wife
	No kids
	No family here
	No Muslim friends
	No Zakat
	No home
	No money
	No Youssef

I leave the notebook back and return to Karim. He is flying to Algiers in the morning. I tell him I'm sorry for barging in earlier.

—I have to start praying again, he says. I have to return to Islam. We never know the hour we'll be called to meet Allah.

Dusk is falling as I walk back to my house. Karim will be calling home now, speaking to his family, one by one, in Arabic. Crying, asking questions, each silently reconstructing Youssef's last minutes. The round of gunfire, the little boy's body falling, then the screech of brakes, the sound of sirens, the long minutes before his mother comes down into the street.

24

KARIM WILL BE away for at least a month. During the first week, I call him every evening, and the call is very brief. How is your family? I ask and I can barely hear his reply. I lie in bed at night with Boo beside me, imagining his days in Algiers – at dinner with his family, at the mosque with his father for Friday prayers, visiting Youssef's grave. A city boy, among his own people again, hurrying along familiar streets, past women in hijabs and children on their way to school and young men congregated at street corners.

At the weekend, I gather Camus's books around me to bring me closer to Algiers and, therefore, Karim. In *The Outsider* I reread the scene on the beach where Meursault is blinded by the sun and the glint of the knife just before he shoots at the Arab. He fires four more shots . . . *and it was there, in that sharp but deafening noise , that it all started . . . And then it was like giving four sharp knocks at the door of unhappiness.*

I reread Camus's essays that recall his childhood years. *That district, that house! . . . He knows he would climb the staircase without stumbling once. He bears this house in his very body.* He bears his mother, too. One evening in the semi-darkness of the apartment he stands watching her, unseen. She is thin and bony, and he feels pity and sorrow for this silent, illiterate woman who is dominated by her own mother – a harsh, overbearing old woman who rules over the household. His mother has never hugged or kissed him, because she wouldn't know how. She is huddled in a chair now, exhausted from her cleaning job, and he, the young Camus, is a little afraid of her. The light outside is fading. Sounds that she cannot hear drift up from the street, but she is gazing at the floor. He feels separate from her, but becomes conscious of her suffering and, in the silence, he experiences an upsurge of feeling that he thinks must be love. Later, he feels compassion for his grandmother too. One evening, as a teenager, when he and the others go to the cinema, he is *confronted by the most atrocious suffering he has ever known: that of a sick old woman left behind by people going to the movies.*

I cannot get enough of Camus. In town, I buy the biography by Herbert Lottman, then the one by Olivier Todd. The following week I find *Algerian Chronicles* in a second-hand bookshop and read Camus's reports of the poverty, the destitution, the colonial injustice meted out by the French authorities in the Kabyle – the famine-stricken, mountainous Berber region – written for an Algerian newspaper beginning in 1939. In a village in the Tizi Ouzou district, Camus comes upon a group of children in rags, fighting with dogs over garbage. Tizi Ouzou – I remember this name; it is where Karim's grandparents came from. Camus's reports are clear and factual, harrowing in their neutral tone. A group of starving women walk forty kilometres in winter to get government handouts of grain. On their way home to their remote villages, many of them freeze to death in the snow. Like the starving poor in the west of Ireland during the Famine, I think. Men, women and children dying in ditches, frozen, their mouths stained green from eating grass. In Tizi Ouzou, Camus writes, at least fifty per cent of the population survived on thistle stems and marrow roots. Forest regulations imposed by the French authorities prohibited people from gathering twigs to light fires. If caught, offenders were punished by having their only possession – an emaciated old donkey, usually – seized. I take a deep breath, try to calm my raging heart. Humankind is an abomination. I gaze at Camus's photograph. Camus was the only Frenchman my father trusted, Karim told me once.

In the Lottman biography I underline street names and landmarks, and then find them on a map online. The Botanical Gardens are still there. The working-class district of Belcourt, where Camus grew up, side by side with Muslims and other pieds-noir children, is now named Belouizdad. A few blocks from rue de Lyon, I find his primary school. The neighbourhood beach, Plage de l'Arsenal, where Camus swam with his friends, is now subsumed into the nearby docklands. Karim and his friends also swam at the beaches of Algiers. Back and forth I go between biography and map. I find Camus's lycée and the University of Algiers, where he studied philosophy. When he first arrived in Paris, Camus found the city cold and grey and lonely. Just like Karim, I think. He missed the sun and the sea and the warmth of the Algerians. I am looking for affinity in the lives of Karim and Camus and finding parallels everywhere. Love of soccer. Pity for the poor. Preoccupation with death. *I am not cut out for politics,* Camus wrote . . . *I am incapable of wanting or accepting the death of the adversary.*

On the map, I move out of the city, west to Tipasa, where the Roman ruins are surrounded by bougainvillaea and hibiscus and the sound of the sea. Here, among the warm stones and with the scent of absinthe and the grandeur of sea and sky, Camus learned to breathe. The sea close by always, the sun and the sky, the limpid day. Everywhere, he sought the sensual pleasures of love and life and landscape. The light at Tipasa. The wind at Djémila. The poignant longing for Algeria and its people, for the return to that paradise. And everywhere, the woes of the poor and the dispossessed weighing on him. At age forty-five he was still moved and distressed by the same things that moved and distressed him at twenty-five. He found the beautiful landscape of the Kabyle almost unbearable to watch. The splendid sea and the night sky brought no comfort to the people of the Kabyle. Starving people cannot eat beauty.

I am consumed by Camus. At night, I spend hours online, trawling through photographs. Here he is, stretched out on the grass with Francine, his wife, and, here, he sits inside a playpen with their twins, Catherine and Jean. On a Paris street, on a theatre stage, at literary events, handsome, elegant, dressed in wool suits and coats, a cigarette between his fingers or lips. On a Paris balcony with María Casares, his mistress. I zoom in and examine his eyes for signs of guilt or shame. These are the eyes of a womaniser, an adulterer, but I see no difference in these eyes than in those of other photos, no signs of shame or regret or remorse. Physical love, Camus said, was always bound to an irresistible feeling of innocence and joy. He fell in love with each woman, unlike Sartre, who simply used women. But what of the women's suffering? Where is Francine's joy? Where is the innocence in deception? How could Camus, who suffered profoundly and had the deepest empathy for humanity's plight, bear to inflict such pain on Francine?

On my screen, a colourised photograph of Camus in a restaurant, his thin arm draped around his friend and publisher, Michel Gallimard. They could be brothers, or lovers. Brought close, from the beginning, by their mutual tubercular condition, and an awareness of death. I have never seen him so happy. In his last years, he is tormented – his beloved Algeria is being torn apart in violence, and he is estranged from old friends. *Algeria obsesses me this morning*, he writes. *Too late, too late . . . My land lost, I would be worth nothing.* On the street one day, he starts to suffocate. He is, he tells a friend, *diminished*.

On the morning of January 4th 1960, Camus left his home in Lourmarin in the south of France to return to Paris, with Michel Gallimard at the wheel. In the back seat were Gallimard's wife, Janine, her eighteen-year-old daughter, Anne, and her little dog. They drove north on Route 5, stopping for lunch along the way. About sixty miles south of Paris, near the town of Villeblevin, Michel Gallimard's sports car spun off the road and slammed against a huge plane tree. In the seconds it took for the car to bounce off that tree and spin and smash into a second tree forty feet away, did Camus realise he was finished? That he, for whom the Greeks meant so much, had finally been caught by the god of death that had haunted him since he was seventeen? Travelling in the front passenger seat, he was thrown backwards when the car hit the second tree and thrust through the rear window, his skull fractured, his neck broken, his death instantaneous.

A night-time photo shows the body of the car wrapped

around the tree, all the wheels missing. Another photo shows the roof buckled, the doors missing, the interior almost empty. The dashboard was flung thirty feet away, debris scattered over a 500-feet radius. A man – perhaps a garage worker – stands there, staring at the wreckage. How was it possible for Janine and Anne to have survived such a crash? Anne was found in a field, sixty-five feet away. Janine was found on the ground near her bleeding husband, in shock, calling for her dog, a Skye terrier named Floc, who was never seen again. The car clock had stopped at 1.54 p.m., the speedometer stuck at 145 kmph. A flat tyre on the Facel Vega HK500, a blow-out at high speed, a broken axle, or the rear wheel blocking were all suggested as likely causes. Michel Gallimard died from his injuries a few days later in a Paris hospital.

Night is sad in the south, Camus had observed to a friend a few weeks before his death. In photo after photo, I find that the wrecked car resembles less a sports car than the black Morris Minor my father owned in the 1960s. I have no memory of the actual car, but it appears in my parents' wedding and honeymoon photographs. My mother, in her white wedding dress and veil, poised beside its open door as if she is about to step into a limousine; the newly-weds on honeymoon in the Ring of Kerry, standing shyly side by side, with the shiny black Morris Minor behind them, their sentinel. Somewhere in my youth I absorbed the knowledge – probably from my father – that the worst thing a car can hit is a tree. There is no *give* in a tree. The impact is sudden and profound. A journalist reported that Camus's eyes were open and his face had the look of horror. His leather briefcase containing his passport, journal, some books and personal photographs, and the manuscript of his unfinished novel, was recovered from the muddy field. His body was moved by the gendarmes to Villeblevin town hall, and his possessions were locked in the mayor's office, and later turned over to his widow. The government sent down an official from Paris. By evening, Francine and her sister Suzy and Suzy's husband had arrived, as had Camus's loyal secretary, Suzanne Agnely, and Camus's friends. His body lay on a cot under a sheet in the main room of the town hall. The clock was stopped and the walls were draped in black. A bouquet of ordinary flowers was placed on the body. Emmanuel Roblès lifted the sheet to look at his friend who, he said, had the expression of a very tired sleeper, and had a long scratch across his forehead 'like a line drawn across a page to strike it out'. The very next morning Camus was in his coffin being driven back down Route 5, to be waked in the house in Lourmarin he'd left not twenty-four hours earlier.

I feel a kind of vertigo, a falling towards the man, as if I myself am now bereaved. Heartsick too, for his loss, for his youth, for the loss to the world of his profound compassion, his intellect, his delicate mind. On the first page of his manuscript, he had written a dedication to his mother: *To you, who will never be able to read this book.* How is that this man — dead for over forty years — can have such an effect on me, that I am made weak and nauseous when I catch sight of his name or his photograph, or when I read his words or his life? Or, simply, when I think of him.

Would I love Karim now if I had not first loved Camus? Would Karim's mention of Algiers and the Kabyle and Tizi Ouzou have evoked this sense of familiarity and longing in me if I had not first encountered those city streets and beaches or heard the winds at Djémila through Camus? There is, in both men, an honesty, an innocence and earnestness — the same kind of innocence and earnestness I find in my father — which causes me to forgive, easily, their failings.

25

PETER KEEPS APPEARING in my path when Karim is away. I turn into an aisle in Tesco on Friday evening, and there he is, halfway down, basket in hand. I slip out of the store and wait in the car park until he has left. I spot him on the street in Terenure or Rathgar regularly, head down, shoulders hunched, and though I am constantly primed to come upon him, I still get a jolt when I see him. Always alone, he appears a little forlorn lately. One afternoon, driving home from school, I recognise his car coming towards me. The street is narrow, with barely enough room for two cars to pass and we slow to a crawl, inching along until we draw level. Then, as if compelled, we both stop. We are barely two feet apart, separated by glass and steel. He lowers his window and gives me a long look. My heart is pounding. I look at him, but do not open my window. I am afraid he will say something, berate me. But he just nods, and slowly smiles. His look is not hostile, but humble, as if acknowledging something. For an instant I might smile back, but I am confused, disconcerted. Then he bows his head, puts the car in gear and edges forward. I am shaken, unnerved by the encounter. When I get home, I call my solicitor to ask why the divorce is taking so long. Peter has been dragging his heels; he has not yet discovered vital documents. As I listen, I realise that I am to blame too – I have been lax, complacent, reluctant to face the inevitable. I instruct her to get tough with Peter's solicitor, get things moving so that I can get on with my life.

Then I call Karim.

—How is your sister? I ask.

—She's grief-stricken. She cannot eat or sleep. But she knows Youssef is with Allah.

He has changed his plans – he is going to stay in Algiers for an extra month, he tells me. He has started to pray again, and he has given up alcohol.

—Are you ever coming back? I ask.

—Of course.

—What about work?

—I can work from here, he says. In the background there's traffic, horns blaring. I can barely hear him.

—Are you out in the street?

—Yes, he says, can you hear me? Hello?

—I miss you, I say.

—I miss you too, Melina, he says.

He had started to call me Melina before he left. Because you are sweet, he said, like a melon.

—When you come back, will you move in with me? I ask.

He laughs. We'll see, he says, and the line breaks up.

At school, a mangey, emaciated fox has started to appear in the yard, disturbed by the building work in the adjoining site and seeking shelter under the hedge. Human and animal suffering everywhere, I think. The principal comes on the intercom and warns the pupils not to approach the fox. In the staffroom she tells the teachers she has engaged a pest control company to come and set a trap. In my one-to-one sessions with the children, they bring up the fox, a mix of curiosity and fear in their voices. Ruth, a gifted, precocious ten year old with an IQ in the ninety-ninth percentile is anxious. She is concerned about the urban foxes who increasingly cross paths with city dwellers. She has watched this fox's comings and goings and thinks it is a vixen who has cubs nearby. Ruth is sensitive to animal suffering, to all suffering. Bored in class and frequently isolated by her peers, she walks around the yard alone at break time. She has the wit and erudition of a bright adult, and she and I bonded from the start. We laugh at each other's stories. She tells me about the latest discoveries in quantum science and astronomy – the names of quantum physicists and Astronomers Royal trip off her tongue. She plays the flute at the school concert and moves every man, woman and child with her rendition of Schubert's 'Ave Maria'.

After a few weeks, the fox has disappeared and is forgotten. In our sessions, I notice that Ruth is preoccupied, quieter than usual, and pale too.

—Is everything okay? I ask.

—Sure, she says, and launches into an account of a programme she watched on the Science Channel. She has a habit of talking in a rapid, almost gleeful fashion that serves to conceal or deflect pain and excuse – even forgive – the cruelty of others.

One Friday evening, I ask again. Is there something on your mind, Ruth? Is something or someone upsetting you?

She becomes a little agitated. Hesitantly, she shows me the remnant of a wart on her little finger, that had been growing slowly for a long time.

—I watched a documentary on Discovery about herbal cures, she says, and if you rub dandelion milk — the juice inside dandelion stems — on warts, it will cure them.

She points out the window to the yard.

—During break time, a few weeks ago, I pulled some dandelions and squeezed the milk out of the stems onto my wart.

—Did that help?

She shrugs. A bit, she says, becoming distressed. Her voice breaks. I threw away the broken stems under the hedge. That was the time the fox was here. And . . . you see, dandelions are poisonous to animals. She can hardly speak. I think the fox ate the dandelions, she whispers. I think I killed the fox.

I shake my head. No, no, Ruth. You didn't kill the fox. The fox was removed — the school had the fox taken away.

We are silent for a long time, neither of us able to move. We hear the final bell and the classes spilling out onto the corridor. Her suffering is immense. Every night for weeks, she has carried this guilt, this worry, imagining the fox's slow death.

I tell her she is the kindest, most sensitive, person I have ever met. I can barely hold back my own tears.

Later, I think of the fox — the trap, the frantic struggle to get to her cubs as the pain and the poison take hold. And the eternal waiting of the cubs.

That evening, I am filled with an old, familiar feeling of foreboding. When darkness falls, I call Karim — ostensibly to tell him about Ruth and the fox, but really just to hear his voice and be reassured – but he does not answer. I lift Boo onto my lap, and we both doze off.

I am awoken by the phone's ringing. It is Mark, Peter's brother. I have not spoken to any member of Peter's family for over four years.

—Where are you? Mark asks.

—I'm at home. What is it?

—Have you someone there with you? he asks.

—No, I'm alone. What's wrong?

Mark pauses for a few seconds.

—Peter went to the Himalayas about ten days ago, he says. He had a fall early this morning. I'm not entirely clear what happened . . . but I'm afraid he's missing.

Boo jumps off my lap and stands in the middle of the floor and tilts her head and looks up at me.

—Anna? Are you there?

—Missing? I can feel my chest tightening, as if a ball is expanding inside it. What happened? I ask.

—I don't know exactly. I don't know his friends, but a man called Tony Malone called me. He was pretty shaken. He said Peter was on an ice climb when it happened.

—Tony Malone used to be his climbing partner. Was he with Peter?

—No, he was back at the camp.

—Where did he fall? Why can't they find him? Are they searching?

—I think they tried, at the start. I couldn't follow everything he said, to be honest, but I gathered conditions are too treacherous to continue searching at the moment. The area is prone to avalanches at this time of year. It sounded like the fall was very steep . . . Tony mentioned a crevasse. It sounded like there's not much hope that Peter could have survived. He's going to call me again in the morning.

I am silent for a moment, trying to picture it, trying to figure it out.

—I don't understand, I say. Was Peter the only one who fell? Was he roped up?

—I don't know . . . He is silent for a few moments. Anna, he says, this is difficult, but I don't think you and Peter are divorced, are you?

—No.

—So, legally, you're Peter's next of kin. I'll have to give your contact details to the Irish Embassy. Is that okay?

—Yes, of course.

I am thinking of all the frozen landscapes that are littered with bodies. It is not uncommon for climbers to come upon one, long-preserved in the snow.

—Anna, are you still there?

—Yes.

—When the weather improves, it may be possible to recover his body. If it can be found.

26

IN THE EARLY years of our marriage Peter had, briefly, become interested in potholing. No sane person could call that a sport, I said, after reading a guide to potholing in County Clare that he'd bought. One weekend, he went down to the Burren on a kind of reconnaissance trip. I knew he might enter a man-sized hole on a forest floor, scramble deep underground, move through channels and passages. I could hardly breathe at the thought of it. In the guide, I studied photographs of men and women wedged in tunnels or crawling along narrow passageways, miners' lamps on their heads, stopping to smile at the camera. Thigh-deep in water in vaulted caves, ropes attached to their waists, and not a hint of fear in their faces. The word *enchanting* was used to describe a world under lush fields and limestone deserts. Something must have happened on that Burren trip to put Peter off, because he remained above ground after that, venturing to greater heights, year after year.

* * *

I call my mother and then Elaine and Fintan, and they all fall silent, stunned at the news. A long silence on the phone, too, when I tell Karim.

—I'm so sorry, Melina, he says eventually.

—I met him on the road just before he went out there – maybe even the day before he left, I say. We were both in our cars and he stopped and looked at me. He wasn't hostile or anything. The way he looked at me was strange . . . As if he had a premonition.

—Life is very strange, Melina.

—When are you coming home, Karim?

—I don't know. In a week or two. Sooner, maybe.

—Please come sooner, if you can. I miss you.

Phone calls, too, the next morning, and emails back and forth with the Irish Embassy in Delhi and calls with Mark all day long. No one can say exactly what happened or what caused the fall. The area they were climbing in was heavily crevassed and later that day there was a report of a small avalanche there.

Online, I bring up images of the Himalayan peaks and search until I find the twin peaks of Nanda Devi, and hover there. Nanda Devi East and Nanda Devi West, separated by a two-kilometre-long ridge. Named for the Goddess of Bliss, this is heavenly earth. Even if Peter never reached either summit, this is the top of the world, the place where elite climbers unknowingly come to die. Climbers themselves sometimes accidentally trigger avalanches and rockfalls. Exhaustion can lead to lapses of concentration, errors of judgment. The dictum is: save yourself. Do not stop for stranded colleagues, and when you are stranded, do not expect help. In the later years of our marriage, Peter read *Touching the Void*, the story of a climber's survival against all odds. In 1985, high in the Peruvian Andes, Joe Simpson dangled precariously at the end of a rope held by his climbing partner, Simon Yates. Simpson had already broken his leg in an earlier incident. As the hours passed, the rope weakened, the ice screw came loose and they both knew they would soon fall to their deaths. Eventually, to save himself, Yates cut the rope and Simpson dropped into a deep crevasse – a black hole with sheer walls that offered no way out other than a slow death or a merciful loss of consciousness. Yates, upset and disturbed, crawled into a snow hole until morning, and then made his way back to base camp. A few nights later, Simpson showed up. Miraculously, he had made his way up out of the crevasse and crawled on his belly along a glacier and down the mountain until he arrived, exhausted, emaciated and hallucinating, a few yards from Yates's tent at base camp.

There is little to do but wait. If there's a window in the weather, the liaison woman at the Irish Embassy tells me, local rescue teams may be deployed to attempt recovery. Later, Mark tells me there'll be a better chance of a visual sighting and recovery in a few months' time when some of the snow melts and reveals its catch. But even as Mark is speaking, I know that these rescue and recovery missions are rare because of the risks and the prohibitive costs. And if Peter fell into a crevasse, then recovery is surely impossible.

—Anna, Mark says . . . Do you know if Peter was seeing anyone? A woman, I mean.

—I don't know, I say. I hadn't spoken to him in a long time.

—He was always secretive, even when he was young. Always

a bit of a loner. You know, in his whole life, you were the only one he was ever close to.

Mark asks me to visit his mother. I have not seen her in years. When she sees me, she lets out a cry and, holding me in a tight embrace, begins to weep.

—Ye should never have split up, she says. He was never the same after that. The poor boy. I think losing the child that time affected him badly . . . Do you think they'll find him, Anna?

Afterwards, Mark and I drive to Peter's house, to check on everything and turn off the water. He has arranged for a locksmith to meet us there and open the door and fit a new lock. As we enter, Mark hands me one of the new keys. We walk around the downstairs rooms, separately, nervously, as if we might open a door and find Peter – or a version of Peter – sitting there. This is the house I first entered with Peter, where I first slept with him. My eyes glance over his possessions. Coats and jackets hanging in the hall. Bills on the kitchen counter. A mug in the sink. He had walked out of here two weeks ago, expecting to come back, but his death was already hovering over him and the countdown had begun. I stand at the sink and look out at the garden and for a few seconds I feel faint and vertiginous as I realise we are all hurtling towards our end. I, too, at this very moment am hurtling towards my end.

—Should we open these? Mark asks, later. He is holding some mail.

—I don't know, I say.

We are standing in the sitting-room, not knowing what to do or say.

—It's strange . . . eerie, being here, isn't it? Mark whispers.

The phone rings on a side table, startling us both. After a few rings, the answering machine switches on. *Please leave a message*, says Peter. But the caller leaves no message. We stand there, shaken. Mark crosses the room and presses the Play button. *No new messages*, the machine says.

I look out on the street. There is no one around – the children are in school, the adults at work.

—He might not be dead, I whisper. He might have survived and still turn up. It happens, you know . . . injured climbers make their way back down.

Mark shakes his head. Not at this stage, he says, his voice breaking. He's gone.

But I have a strong impression of Peter still. If he had died, I am certain I would, at the moment of death, have felt something – a death knock, a presentiment. He might, right now, be dragging himself like Joe Simpson through snow and ice, to soon arrive, like an apparition, back at the camp. I do not believe you are dead, I think. Until I see your body with my own eyes, I will not believe.

27

I RETURN TO Peter's house, alone, the next day, almost eighteen years after I first entered it. The furniture and carpets have changed, the colour of the walls too. In the kitchen, I stare at Peter's mug, at the dried-in tea stain on the bottom, and the smudge from his lips near the rim. I wash and dry the mug and put it away, then pour myself a glass of water and stand looking out at the tree and for a second, I am back in that time, back in his universe, waiting for the sound of his key in the front door.

Upstairs, in the boxroom, there's a computer on his desk and files stacked neatly on bookshelves. In the bathroom, the bath has been replaced by a shower. A red towel hangs on a rail above the radiator. I push open the door of the guest bedroom. On the bed sits an assortment of climbing equipment – multicoloured ropes, a well-worn harness that holds the shape of Peter's backside, a sling, a plastic box containing carabiners and belay devices. On the floor, hiking boots, a pair of blue climbing shoes, a set of crampons. I remember a photograph from the Himalayan trip he took years ago, how it seemed as if he was walking vertically up a sheer ice face, wearing crampons and carrying an ice hammer in each hand. Another box on the floor contains an ice axe and ice screws. I pick up an ice screw, surprised at its solidity and weight. I remember *Touching the Void* again — it is all I have to go on, to conjure up a picture. Ice screws provide anchors for the climber, Peter explained once, and must be placed in the ice at a very particular angle. The quality of the ice is critical too — a climber must be able to recognise weakened ice, because an ice screw must bear his weight if he falls.

When I enter Peter's bedroom, I get his scent — his ordinary human scent, faintly sweaty, still living in the fibres of his sheets and duvet and pillows. In the wardrobe, his jackets and shirts and trousers, his jumpers folded on shelves. I reach up and far back on the high shelf, but there is no velvet box, no pixie-girl ring.

Something rattles downstairs and my heart almost stops, and I freeze. What if he walks in and finds me here, trespassing? What if there *is* a woman, and she's downstairs, trying to enter with her old key? I wait, and when nothing more happens, I cross to the window. A postman is wheeling his bicycle along the footpath, then he stops and leaves it against a pillar. I look across at the other houses, almost identical to this. All the lives being lived since my first night here, the Sunday morning when I heard the children coming out to play.

Suddenly, I am ambushed by grief. For Peter, for the life we might have lived, for the children we might have had. I sit on the floor and lean against the bed. He is dead. He is dead and I am still afraid. I begin to imagine his fall. The sudden sensation in the body. The darkening of light, the breaking of bones, the crushing of organs. The descent into a crevasse, then the silence. He might have survived. He might have remained alive in the darkness, injured, terrified, but straining, fighting to find a way through, until reason and the life force ebbed away. How long does it take to die? Drifting in and out of consciousness, visited by dreams, visions, hallucinations. How long before the mind tumbles down into itself?

Slowly, it begins to dawn on me: Peter was always vulnerable, always endangered. He was a wounded man, a wounded boy — the smallest criticism injured him deeply. It is why he never wanted to be fully known or *seen*, and why self-examination was anathema to him. What was he afraid of? That, if he looked deep, he would find little of value, or worse . . . nothing? I am *trying* to understand. Was it all a matter of self-preservation for Peter? Did he need to keep parts of himself sealed off to prevent someone getting too close and infringing upon his life and his mind — to prevent *me* from getting too close, from gazing at his soul? Was he afraid that the fragile self would be exposed, and found wanting, and the pain of such exposure would be annihilating? His fear was surely unconscious but, still, manifest. For a few terrible moments I realise that *I* represented a threat to Peter's psyche, a threat so great that, in an act of self-preservation, he was forced to sabotage our relationship. The philandering was not just a search for love or validation, but an unconscious attempt to escape, to save himself. I should have known this, I should have understood that he fled because he could not look inwards, he could not become conscious. But there is no escaping the unconscious. How could he have known that his flight would, in the end, be futile, and all the gallivanting, all the running and swimming and climbing, all the unconscious appetites and instincts would lead, ultimately, to this moment: his obliteration, his total annihilation.

I get into his bed, pull the duvet over my head and close my eyes. I see him perched precariously on a narrow ledge deep in a crevasse. Paralysed in eternal darkness. Thousands of miles from home, from his mother and brothers, from his child's grave. We are all flesh, and death is approaching. It is coming for me too, announcing itself in my nervous system, warning me that I, too, am floating close to hazard, that I, too, am only a hair's breadth from disaster, and there is no knowing the day or the hour or the minute.

I flee that house in panic. On the way home, cars come at me from every direction, huge trucks bear down on me, their horns blaring. In the kitchen I put away all the knives, lock all the windows and doors and put on the alarm. Peter's death has imperilled me. All evening, I move around the house, full of fear, unable to anchor myself. I become fixated on the electrical system, picturing the cables that crisscross the attic floor, imagining them worn and bare where they intersect, where live wires will spark and ignite while I sleep. I call Karim and leave a message, begging him to come home. Boo watches me from her bed. Finally, I sit in the dining-room and stare at the little pile of books on the table. *Islam in Focus.* Karen Armstrong's *Mohammed.* The Qur'an. Trust in God, Karim said, and you will never be afraid.

I open the Qur'an and begin to read and, slowly, the terror begins to ease. I read carefully, line by line, surah after surah, whispering the words until, gradually, I grow calm. When the night comes down, I switch on the computer and listen to the adhan, and my heart swells. The call to prayer can be heard on the moon, Karim had said. I listen to it over and over, and in its plaintive sound, I feel the approach of God.

I lift the Qur'an again and turn a page. *If you loan to Allah a beautiful loan, He will double it to your credit, And He will grant you Forgiveness.*

28

I AM ENTHRALLED by everything I read about Islam, everything I learn, and slowly I am relieved of the weight of the world. The pen traces the name of God on the page, I read. The water-skater, in its haphazard movements, traces His name on the surface of water. Everywhere I turn, I am fortified. I walk Boo on Sandymount Strand and the tide flows over my feet in gentle ripples and a flock of geese flies above me in a V-shaped formation, and it is as if I am seeing seawater and birds and sky for the first time.

I watch videos on how to do wudu – ablution before prayers. I wash my hands up to the wrist, three times. Three times I rinse out my mouth and nose, wash my face three times with both hands, from top to bottom and ear to ear. Next, the right hand is washed up to the elbow, followed by the left, three times each. The whole head must be wiped with wet hands, then the inside of the ears. Finally, the feet, up to the ankles, beginning with the right foot, three times each. Ablution stays valid until the next prayer unless one uses the toilet, sleeps, bleeds, has sexual intercourse or takes medication.

Karim is ecstatic when I tell him on the phone.

—Masha'Allah, he says, this is the best news, Melina! You are a Muslim! I am so happy for you, so proud of you. I cannot wait to see you. One more week and I will be there.

Every night, I follow online lessons and, slowly, I learn how to perform prayer. I love the names of the prayers, their sounds – Fajr, the prayer at sunrise, and Maghrib, at sunset, are my favourites. They must all be said in Arabic, so when the teacher pronounces the words, I read them and repeat them aloud, phonetically, and practise them over and over, stopping and starting the video, until I learn off one line, then the next. I stand and place my right hand over my left, above my navel, in the Wuquf position; then as the prayer proceeds I bow in the Ru'ku position, then prostrate myself for Sujud and rest back on my heels for the Jalsa position. With a compass I find the direction of Mecca, 5,000 kilometres away and at an angle of 118 degrees, and reorientate myself daily to the Qibla.

I download the daily prayer timetable for Dublin from the Islamic Centre's website and, five times a day, I lay a clean towel on my bedroom floor, put on a long dressinggown, cover my hair with a headscarf, knotted at the back, and perform my prayer. At night I stand in the back garden looking up at the moon, feeling its light, its orbit – *being* its orbit – out there in empty space. A Hebrew word, Ziv, comes to mind, the unearthly light of God's presence. Then a siren sounds in the distance, or a dog barks, or a cheer goes up in a nearby house during a football match — and all of these elements elevate the moon, reflect its brilliant light back to me. God has shown me all this, restored to me this incandescent moon, this incandescent life.

When Karim returns, he brings me a prayer rug and a small leather-bound Qur'an, and when I open it and see the border ornamentation in red and blue on the title page, I am rooted to the spot. The dream from years ago — where I am in the park and receive a phone call from Ahmad — returns. This is the decorated page that appeared in that dream. I am rocked to my core at the realisation that Karim was predicted in that dream, that Islam was sanctioned.

With Karim as my witness, I say the Shahada, my declaration of faith. Afterwards, we walk in the Botanic Gardens, like we did in the early days.

—Listen, Karim says, listen to the birds praising God. And today they are praising Melina too! Now you will never be afraid again, you will have peace and tranquillity because Allah will guide you.

Karim gives notice to his landlord and, a month later, moves in with me, and I sleep with ease now. Even Boo, who has been relegated from the bedroom to the kitchen at night, makes no objection. On this clear path, I am learning and accepting that everything has a place and a purpose and a meaning. I rise for Fajr prayer at 3 a.m. while Karim sleeps on. I do wudu and bow and pray and, in the dead of these nights, I have never felt closer to God. Karim is moved by my commitment. You are a better Muslim than I am, he says. He has a satellite dish installed on the roof so he can receive Al Jazeera and other Arabic channels. After school, I walk Boo in the park and I see now that every flower, every tree, is bowing down to Allah. Afterwards, I do wudu and combine the Zuhr and Asr prayers, and then read a page from the Qur'an. When Karim gets home, we prepare dinner. I see how gently he chops the vegetables and cooks the food. It is the way he does everything – prayerfully, with love.

—If we cook with anger or hostility, he says, the food will be no good.

There is a way to do everything, and in this simple, ordered life of work and prayer and sleep, I have never been happier.

Every night, after watching Channel Four News we switch to the Islam Channel, where, at 8 p.m., an imam answers viewers' questions live on air. The calls come from all over the UK and Europe. One night, a Dublin man phones in. He is a recent convert to Islam, and he is, he says, distressed by the teachings on the punishment in the grave. The Sunnah, he says, states that, after death, non-Muslims and Muslim sinners are crushed in their graves, and this torment will endure until Judgment Day and every minute will feel like an eternity.

—Why, the Dublin man asks, are people who have never encountered Islam punished? My mother died last month, he says, his voice breaking. She knew nothing about Islam. She is innocent! Is she now suffering in her grave?

—Brother, the imam says softly, this is from the Hadith, the teachings and practices of Mohammed, Peace Be Upon Him. The Prophet's own father suffers in the grave – not even the Prophet's father is spared! This is why we must do da'wah and call our loved ones – all our fellow men and women, all our compatriots – to Islam.

I shake my head and look at Karim.

—That can't be right, I say. Surely those teachings are not meant to be interpreted literally – as *physical* punishment. Surely they're metaphorical – the pain is abstract, like longing or loneliness. And, anyhow, not everyone ends up in an *actual* grave.

Karim frowns. No, Melina, the punishment in the grave is real. It's why I keep saying you must invite your family to Islam, you *have* to tell them about Islam.

—But it's a Hadith, it's not in the Qur'an.

He looks at me, appealing. You must tell them, he says.

I get up and walk into the kitchen, rattled. I think of my grandmother in her grave, and my uncle who died in a car crash before I was born. And Peter, and the child. All children go straight to heaven, Karim told me when Youssef died.

That night, online, I learn that there are ninety-nine names for Allah, and I download the list, and learn off the first eight names by heart. I think of the Dublin man, out there in the city somewhere. In the next street, maybe, the next house. My brother in faith.

Every day I learn off four more of Allah's names. Allah, the Most Merciful. The Giver of Gifts. The All-Aware. The Absolute Pure. On Saturday, we go to the mosque in Clonskeagh. Karim goes to the men's area to do wudu and perform his prayer, and I enter the women's area. There is a row of sinks by a wall where two women are doing wudu, and a seating area with books and toys where mothers with small children are gathered. Several women smile and say, Hello, sister. I nod and smile back. But I feel sick, frightened, out of my depth. I do not belong here. Beyond the window, I can see a patio and garden area, but no door leads out there. I turn around and exit quickly. I hurry along the corridors, afraid I will meet someone I know — a family from school maybe — and return, in panic, to the car. What am I doing here, I think, these are not my people. It is as if I have wandered into alien territory. I think of Boo at home and long to be with her.

And then I see Karim crossing the car park, and my heart lifts. The sight of him — or just the thought of him — always recovers me. We go back inside and have lunch in the restaurant, then browse in the shop. He buys me a book, *Invocations and Supplications,* by the twelfth-century scholar, Al-Ghazali, and a hijab that can be slipped on over the head for prayers.

—It would be nice if you wore it in public too, he says.

When I make no reply, he adds, In time, of course.

And I think, yes, in time, I will be brave.

29

MARK HAS BEEN taking care of Peter's house and business affairs in the months since his disappearance. He accompanies me to a meeting with Peter's solicitor who informs us that if, after a few months, Peter's body is not found, she will apply to the Courts for a presumption of death order, but cautioned that it may not succeed because a person must be missing for seven years before such an order can be granted. However, she will plead that Peter's case is different from the usual missing persons' cases, but she will need evidence and documentation from the Indian authorities, and statements from mountain rescue and other climbers – anything that can help to support our claim that Peter's fall was fatal. Outside, afterwards, Mark says, We have to accept that Peter is dead, Anna.

On the way home, I put on a CD of Qur'anic recitations that Karim gave me. The Qur'an is meant to be chanted, he said. It is like music, the chanting slows you down. Once, when he was a teenager, Karim was on a crowded bus in Algiers during a heatwave and saw the evidence of this. There was no air-conditioning, and tempers were frayed and passengers complained and fought over seats. Then the bus driver put the Qur'an on the speaker and the passengers relaxed and stopped fighting, and the bus grew quiet. There is compassion in the sound of the chanting, Karim said.

I am living a secret life. From the outside, no one can tell I am a Muslim, and no one must ever find out. They would not understand – they would think I was coerced into converting by Karim. I visit my parents less frequently and, when I do and when prayer time arrives, I slip upstairs, do wudu, lock my bedroom door, and don my dressinggown and hijab. As I pray, I am on high alert, listening out for my mother's footsteps on the stairs and, if I hear her approach, I fling off the hijab and dressinggown, my heart in flight, waiting for a call or a knock on the door. It is wrong to hide Allah, and I am heartsick at this concealment. I read that, on Judgment Day, every limb and every organ of this body will testify before Allah. My hands will tell of every deed they ever performed; my feet will reveal every step I took; my eyes and ears will account for every sight and sound they were party to.

—How can you not tell your family about Islam, Karim says. It's cruel. Look at what happened to your husband, and to Youssef. We never know when our hour will come.

I have given up alcohol, but, still, when we eat out and delicious food arrives, I have a great longing for red wine to accompany it. For a few moments I feel a pang of loss for a pleasure that is gone forever, but I say the Shahada silently and, in no time at all, the longing passes. On the drive to school or walking in the park, I recite Allah's names, learning four more on the list every night. Allah, the All-Hearing, the All-Seeing. The Most Kind. The Utterly Just. Where once the lines of Eliot's *The Waste Land* would break me, now Allah's names or Rumi's poetry uplifts me. I no longer read novels, or listen to music – Karim tells me most of these are haram. Instead, I read Louis Massignon on the science of compassion, and articles on Islam by learned scholars. I order Massignon's biography, *The Crucible of Compassion*, and several volumes of Al-Ghazali's *The Revival of the Religious Sciences* series. There is, I learn, a prayer for every imaginable action, every occasion – when looking in a mirror, even, or entering the bathroom, or putting on a new garment. Or, simply, when it rains.

One Sunday in spring, we are having coffee and cake on the terrace café of Powerscourt House in Wicklow. All around us, the magnificent gardens, the forests, the mountains. Nothing to do but give thanks for such splendour. Occasionally, the thought of Peter – Peter's soul – intrudes, and, momentarily, I feel a slight panic rising, the resurrection of old fears, new terrors.

Later, on the way home, when we're stopped at the traffic lights at Lamb's Cross on the outskirts of the city, my eyes alight on a horse and buggy tied to a lamppost outside a newsagent's. The horse is old and thin, and is wearing blinkers. There's an open sore on its hind leg, red and raw and weeping. Before the lights change, two boys, aged about twelve or thirteen – out from the city for a jaunt – emerge from the shop, untie the reins and climb up on the buggy. The horse limps as they set off but, still, one of the boys strikes it with a stick and keeps lashing until the horse is trotting, then galloping. Images and memories come flooding, and the old animal pain rises. All that I have kept at bay now returns. The laboratories, the factory farms, the hunting, the bear-baiting. My father, into whose fields and cattle sheds I can no longer wander, such is the pain. The lights change and we turn left, but the horse remains with me, invading my mind. I mentally track its route back to the city, the clip-clop of its hooves on the streets. The obedient, exhausted body, hungry, thirsty, limping, the iron bit in its mouth chafing its tongue and palate, the silent suffering all day long. I close my eyes but I cannot exit the horse's mind.

That night, I bring it up with Karim.

—Did you see that horse today, at the traffic lights, with the young lads?

He shakes his head.

—He had a wound, an open sore, on his leg. He was limping, in pain. I keep looking at Karim, as if he can help.

—I told you, Melina, Allah knows what's best for all of us.

—You know it's not right, I say, how we treat animals.

Karim makes a face. This is wrong, you know, he says. Allah knows what's best for all creation, for animals too. You shouldn't question Him. He gives you their meat – halal meat, blessed meat – but still you refuse to eat it. And yet you feed it to your dog! He shakes his head. If you *really* trusted in Allah, Melina, you would not say these things. And I told you – the last thing the animal hears before it's slain in the abattoir is Allah's name, whispered in its ear.

He is silent for a few moments, but he is not finished.

—And you should not keep a dog in the house, he says angrily. You know it's haram – I told you it's haram.

I am no longer listening. Last Sunday, when I arrived back from Galway earlier than planned, Boo was out in the back garden.

—How long has she been out there? I asked Karim, after I brought her in.

—About ten minutes, he said.

I didn't believe him. I wanted to ask where in the Qur'an it states that a dog in the house is haram. I wanted to say, It is you, Karim, and not Islam, who made this rule. You and other men like you. I sat on the armchair and took Boo into my arms that evening. When I leaned down and kissed her, she licked my face.

Karim looked away in disgust. Don't kiss me, he said, after kissing your dog.

30

THE HEADACHE STARTS at around noon and grows and intensifies until, by 3 p.m., it is pounding. The Ramadan headache, Karim calls it. It'll be gone in a few days, he says. Between sunrise – which is about 7.15 a.m. these mornings – and sunset – 7.30 p.m. – nothing can pass the lips. Not a sip of water, or a paracetamol tablet, or a puff of a cigarette. The fast will be longer in the coming years when Ramadan falls at the height of summer and fasting starts at 5 a.m. and lasts until 10 p.m. In the staffroom, at lunchtime, I pour a cup of tea, bring it to my mouth and pretend to sip. In the toilet mirror, I look pale and tired. The day drags on interminably. It is so hard, this fasting, that I want to cry. After school, I perform my prayers, feed and walk Boo, then go to bed and count the hours until sunset.

—The first Ramadan is the hardest, Karim says. You'll get used to it and, in winter, when the days are short and the fast breaks around 4 p.m., it will be much easier.

There is a whole month of this fasting. When Karim gets home each evening, he prepares the Iftar meal. Weak and exhausted, I watch the six o'clock news. I keep checking the clock, watching time tick slowly by. When the exact minute arrives, we break the fast with juicy Medjool dates and a glass of water. Such elation! Such gratitude for food and drink! Love for the world, too. After Maghrib prayer, I make a pot of coffee and toast, spread thickly with marmalade – the meal I have longed for all day. Nothing ever tasted so good.

Karim is right. The headache disappears after a few days. I am learning patience. Day by day, the hunger and thirst diminish, and with each evening and each breaking of the fast, the blessings multiply. Joy and understanding increases. Benevolence for all of mankind. Still, I count the days until my period arrives and I am exempt from fasting for its duration but must make up those days again before next year's Ramadan. But even as I wait for sunset, it is as if I am washed clean by this fasting and prayer. From the outside, no one can tell what I'm doing, no one can see this life of order and routine and fulfilment. No one can see my private devotion to God.

It is almost a year since Peter's disappearance and Mark wants to discuss Peter's affairs, so we meet in a café in town. He has a great need to talk about Peter – he tells me stories from their childhood, and bemoans their frequent estrangements in adulthood. I listen and pretend to sip mint tea. Finally, he takes out some documents from a folder.

—I've sorted as much as I can, he says. But, as his wife, you'll have to handle things from now on.

He shows me a letter from Peter's solicitor stating that she has applied to the Courts for a presumption of death order.

—From the bank statements and correspondence I found,

it looks like Peter remortgaged the house two years ago and used the money to buy shares in an offshore gas exploration company.

—Shares? I say. He never invested in shares before.

—That's what I thought too, Mark says. Peter was always quite risk-averse. And the bad news is that the value of those shares has since plummeted.

—That's so odd, so unlike Peter.

—He did have mortgage protection and life cover, but because he died in a climbing accident – climbing is considered a dangerous activity – he's not covered. I checked with his climbing club, and he only took out partial insurance for that trip – medical cover, the cost of being flown home in the event of a medical emergency. Unfortunately, along with his assets, as his wife, you're going to inherit his debts . . . There's only the mortgage and, so far, there's been enough money in his bank account to keep up repayments for the past year. But that money will soon be gone and . . . you'll need to decide what to do.

Weak from fasting, I am overwhelmed now by the thought of these new responsibilities.

—You could sell the house and clear the mortgage, Mark says. That's one option. At current property values you'd probably have a bit left over – twenty or thirty thousand maybe. Or you could let the house, and the rent you'd receive would just about cover the monthly mortgage repayments, so things could tick over. However, that rent would be taxed. If you could manage that – if you could afford to pay tax on the rental income – then at least, in time, the mortgage would be paid and you'd own that second property.

I nod. My mouth is dry and I long for a sip of the mint tea.

—You'll have to take out probate once the death cert is issued. So you'll need to talk to Martina about that – or get your own solicitor. He stops and looks at me for a moment. It's tough, Anna, I know. And I'm aware you need to move on with your life.

—I'll probably sell the house, I say. I want a quiet life. I don't want to have to deal with tenants.

—Well, maybe have a think about it, he says. You could talk to the bank and ask them to pause the repayments until probate is granted so that the mortgage doesn't fall into arrears.

That evening, when Karim arrives home, he unloads heavy wooden panels and begins to assemble them on the back patio. My heart sinks. It is a kennel for Boo.

—What's this? I ask. The birds are singing in the trees behind me.

—It's Ramadan, Melina. We cannot have the dog inside, and you know it. The dog is haram. The dog is unclean.

He takes Boo's bed from the kitchen and puts it inside the kennel, then fits the roof on top. At the front, there's a Perspex flap for entry and exit.

I follow him into the kitchen where he washes his hands.

—She's never stayed outside in her life, I say. She won't be safe. She'll be frightened at night.

—She'll be fine. Most dogs live outside. You're a Muslim now, Melina. You cannot be putting your dog first.

—I'm not putting her first. She's an innocent animal, and she's getting old. She'll think I'm punishing her. Please, Karim.

I am standing in the garden, watching him give a final check to the kennel. The birds are still singing. I feel a great homesickness. I feel far from everything I once knew, exiled from everyone I love.

He looks at me before he goes inside.

—I cannot stay in this house if you bring that dog in again.

Boo will not enter the kennel. I bring out her food and water, but all evening long she sits in the middle of the garden, staring at the back door. As darkness falls, it begins to rain. In desperation, I go out and attach a wooden clothes peg to each side of the kennel flap to keep it propped open, and I leave a treat inside on her bed. Finally, cautiously, she enters. When I go to bed, I cannot sleep. All night long, I am with Boo inside the kennel, her confused, bewildered little eyes staring anxiously out at the garden.

When Ramadan ends, I put Boo in the car, and we head to Killiney beach. As I drive through Churchtown and up Taney Road – the sun dazzling, the trees in leaf again – Van Morrison comes on the radio singing 'Days Like This'. I tap my fingers on the steering wheel to the beat of the song and start to sing along. When I crest the hill on Mount Anville Road, Van begins a solo on the saxophone, and the sea comes into view. A ship sails towards port and, out beyond Howth Head, the pale blue sky dips to the horizon and I am arrested by this beauty, this sun and sky and sea. I remember Camus again and I am filled with an ache, a feeling of insurmountable loss. I can no longer read his novels. Everything I once loved is now haram, and even the beauty of this day is pierced with sadness by all that is forbidden in this new life I have chosen. Boo lifts her head and I leave my hand on her back, and she sighs contentedly. I take a deep breath, recite the Shahada, and drive on.

31

KARIM INSISTS THAT Boo is happier outside. It is summer, and I relent. I chase her around the garden, and she rolls over on the grass for her tickles. When the weather gets cold, I promise her, I'll bring you inside. But then autumn comes, and then winter, and each time I bring it up, Karim frowns and shakes his head.

—You must put your trust in Allah, he says.

In a builders' providers, I buy thick sheets of insulation, cut to size, and line the floor and the walls of the kennel with them. Then I spread an old duvet and two blankets under her bed. I'll make you nice and cosy, I tell her.

The early winter is, mercifully, mild. Before Karim comes home every day, I bring Boo into the living-room and we lie on the floor and it is, briefly, like old times. She is almost ten now, and she's slowing up on her walks. I worry about her — some days she has no appetite — so I take her to the vet. After a full battery of blood tests, the vet tells me her liver function is a bit low.

—It's not unusual in older dogs, he says, but we'll keep an eye on this.

In February, the temperature plummets to below zero, and snow falls overnight. I open the back door in the morning and, nervously, lift the flap of the kennel. Boo raises her sleepy head and comes out and stretches her long body. I bring her inside and feed her before we set off for the park.

—I've been thinking of applying for a job in London, Karim announces one evening. I might send my CV to a few recruitment agencies there.

I am taken aback. Why? I ask.

He shrugs. Just to test the water. I've been with Intel for almost six years now — it's time for a change.

—But why London? Are you not happy here?

—I think it would be good for us, Melina, he says, for you and me. We'd have a better life, a closer community with other Muslims. And with my sister there, you wouldn't be as isolated — she'd be a good friend to you.

—I'm not isolated, I say. Why do you say I'm isolated?

—You're practising your faith in secret, Melina, he says softly. That's not right, you know. You should be proud to declare you're a Muslim. You should be doing da'wah — telling everyone about Islam . . . In London, you'd feel freer.

I could not uproot Boo, I want to say. Instead, I say, I'd miss my family.

—It's only a short flight away. You could visit them often.

During our marriage, Peter and I visited London a few times. I loved the buzz of the city, the museums, the cafés, the parks.

The bookshops and galleries. Eating out in restaurants. In the Tube, being ferried along underground in the great swell of humanity, thinking about what it all meant, metaphorically, metaphysically. I used to dream of living in a big city – London or New York. New York, especially – I would have liked to spend some time there.

Karim is smiling, and I smile back. I start to picture us in London. Boo would get used to it. We could find a place close to a park. Karim is right. We would get to know other like-minded Muslims. I could live a truer life, a more honest life.

— Let's go for a few days – after Ramadan, I say. I'll ask Sinéad to take Boo.

The idea grows on me. I start to look up property to rent, then property for sale, starting in West London – in Hammersmith, because that is where Peter and I once stayed. If we liked London, we could sell this house, buy a place there. Every evening, I'm online, searching property sites, admiring, daydreaming.

But as Ramadan approaches again, I feel a low-level dread. This month-long fast will return, year after year, for the rest of my life. It will be relentless. For eleven months every year, as I wait for it to come round, it will cast a shadow over every other month.

Then Ramadan begins, and when I break the fast each evening, I am restored, made whole again. I could live in London – or anywhere – with Allah's blessing.

32

OUR HOTEL IS in Earl's Court and we take a bus out to Chiswick to visit Karim's sister, Nadia, her husband Samir and their seven-year-old daughter, Fatima. Karim kisses each of them on the cheek and holds Nadia in a long embrace. She is beautiful, with dark hair and sparkling eyes. They all speak Arabic or dialect, then revert to English. Karim has brought gifts for Fatima — a doll, books, colouring pencils — and I have brought flowers and chocolates for Nadia. The child has been kept home from school today in honour of our visit, and Samir has taken a half-day off work. The table is laden with delicious food which Nadia has cooked. Samir is soft-spoken, reserved, and at one point he excuses himself and I am certain he has gone to another room to pray. Karim and Nadia talk about their parents, their sister, Youssef, frequently lapsing into Arabic when they forget I am here. At the table, I can barely eat. I smile at Fatima and ask her about school, and the afternoon passes in a kind of heightened, nervous state.

* * *

Early the next day, we take a bus to London Central Mosque near Regent's Park. We wander around the huge complex, then visit the shop. When the adhan sounds, we part and I go upstairs to the female area. There are dozens of women of all nationalities here, but I am the only one whose head is not covered. I do wudu at the wash area, then take my hijab from my bag and slip it over my head, aware that the other women are watching me. I am even more uncomfortable here than I was in the mosque in Clonskeagh. I see a sign for the women's prayer room at the far end, and as I am about to move, the woman beside me touches my arm.

—Are you okay, sister? Would you like some help? She smiles warmly. I am Aisha, she says.

—Ah, named for the Prophet's wife, I say, the first thing that comes into my head.

—Yes, Suban'atallah. Are you new here?

—I'm visiting from Ireland – with my husband. The first lie of the day.

—You are very welcome. I will show you where to pray.

She takes her prayer rug and we go next door to the women's prayer room and remove our shoes before entering. The red carpet is patterned with individual prayer spaces and we take positions, side by side, in the second row. There is a glass partition at the front, and I can see the main room below, where the men are coming and going and praying with their backs to us. Around us, women arrive and pray, then sit chatting in low tones, with babies in their arms or small children beside them.

Aisha and I stand side by side, and perform our prayer in silence.

Afterwards, I feel calm and more trusting. I tell Aisha I'm a recent convert.

—Insha'Allah, she says, it is a blessing. May your rewards be many.

She is a kindergarten teacher and lives in Shepherd's Bush.

—My husband is French, I say. Well, French-Algerian. The second lie. We might be moving to London soon, I blurt out.

—Insha'Allah, she exclaims. I will give you my phone number. You must stay in touch.

The next morning Karim goes to meet friends and I roam around Covent Garden, pleased to have this time alone in the city. In the National Gallery I go straight to the Van Gogh room and stand before *Sunflowers* for a long time, like I did on my very first visit here years ago. Downstairs, in the café, I buy coffee and a blueberry muffin and sit under a high window where the sun streams in. I am retracing my steps, replicating what I did on previous trips. Afterwards, I walk up to Piccadilly Circus and enter HMV. Maybe it's the hit from the caffeine or the buzz of the city but, as soon as I pass through the entrance, the thump and volume of the music resound in me, sending first a quivering excitement, then a pumped-up feeling through me as I move along the aisles. I am drawn, automatically, to familiar CDs that sit on my shelves at home – Van Morrison, Leonard Cohen, Miles Davis, Billie Holliday, Keith Jarrett – as if to confirm they are real and were always real and still exist in the world. I bring *Astral Weeks* to a playing post and put on the headphones. When Van starts to sing, I close my eyes. It is as if I'm returning home from another planet. I play snippets of 'Sweet Thing', 'Madame

George', 'Ballerina'. In song after song, the old, familiar mystery and magic unfold again and the mood and the memory of the first time I played this album comes unbidden. It was years ago, and Peter and I were on holiday in West Cork, renting a house high up above the village of Rosscarbery with a view out to sea. Every morning Peter went off hiking on the mountains and, all day long, I read and listened to these songs over and over. In the evenings, I prepared dinner and waited, joyously, for Peter's return. So much happiness then. I bring more Van Morrison CDs to the playing post. 'Into the Mystic'. 'And It Stoned Me'. When I play 'Days Like This', I am hit by another memory – driving up Mount Anville Road after Ramadan last year and cresting the hill and seeing Dublin Bay come into view and the feeling – the unbearable feeling – of loss I felt for all I had forsaken.

I stroll along Charing Cross Road and Tottenham Court Road, stopping at the bookstands outside second-hand bookshops. Inside, I browse the shelves of poetry, fiction, religion. I search in vain for books by Al-Ghazali. I buy *Islam and the Destiny of Man* by Gai Eaton, a British diplomat who converted to Islam. I flick through Jung's *Memories, Dreams, Reflections* and suddenly realise that I have not had any dreams – or any that I remember – for a long time. In the fiction section, I find Camus's *The Outsider* and sit on a footstool in a quiet corner. As soon as I read the opening words – words I will know forever – I am back with Camus, back in his whole, moving existence. I turn the pages, searching for the scene where Meursault meets his old neighbour, Salamano, on the stairs with his poor mangey dog. I read:

They look as if they belong to the same species, and yet they hate each other. Twice a day, at eleven o'clock and six, the old man takes his dog for a walk. In eight years they haven't changed their route. You can see them in the rue de Lyon, the dog dragging the man along until old Salamano stumbles. Then he beats the dog and swears at it. The dog cringes in fear and trails behind. At that point it's the old man's turn to drag it along. When the dog forgets, it starts pulling its master along again and gets beaten and sworn at again. Then they both stop on the pavement and stare at each other, the dog in terror, the man in hatred. It's like that every day. When the dog wants to urinate, the old man won't give it time and drags it on, so that the spaniel scatters a trail of little drops behind it. But if the dog does it in the room, it gets beaten again. It's been going on like this for eight years. Céleste always says, 'It's dreadful,' but in fact you can never tell. When I met him on the stairs, Salamano was busy swearing at the dog. He was saying, 'Filthy, lousy animal!' and the dog was whimpering. I said, 'Good evening,' but the old man went on swearing. So I asked him what the dog had done. He didn't answer. He just went on saying, 'Filthy, lousy animal!' I could just about see him, bent over his dog, busy fiddling with something on its collar. I asked him again a bit louder. Then, without turning round, he answered with a sort of suppressed fury, 'He's always there.' Then he set off, dragging the animal after him as it trailed its feet along the grounded, whimpering.

I am convinced, as I was when I first read it, that Camus knew this Salamano character, that he lived in the building in rue de Lyon where Camus grew up, and that this scene really occurred. I read a few more pages, then buy the book and put it in my bag. Out on the street, a little dazzled and disorientated, I hug the bag close to my body, and walk back the way I have come. I pass tables on the footpath, fleet-footed waiters holding trays aloft, diners lifting forkfuls of food to their mouths and sipping sparkling water or wine. A woman throws her head back and laughs and I am amazed at her poise and ease and her carefree laugh. She is in her late thirties, well-dressed, with sunglasses in her long, dark hair. She is eating pasta. She is utterly free, without rules or regulations or prohibitions. Her glass of red wine stands beside her plate. I long for her life, for her sunny, sidewalk seat, for her pasta and red wine, and I have to fight the impulse to reach out my hand, pick up her glass and drink down her wine.

We have a 4.30 p.m. appointment to view a flat for sale in Hamlet Gardens, W6. We arrive early and stroll around the nearby Ravenscourt Park, laid out in lawns and paths and circular flower-beds. We sit on a bench in the shade of an old chestnut tree whose roots, huge and thick and gnarled, radiate out above ground. Dog walkers, and women and children with school bags and sports gear pass by and, from the playground, comes the sound of children playing. Now and then, a woman in a hijab goes by with her children, and I give her a friendly nod. The sunlight flickers through the leaves and falls in patches on the footpath, and I feel an immense peace sitting here under these trees.

In a redbrick 1930s mansion building, the estate agent leads us up to the second floor and into a flat that smells of fresh paint. Off the hall is a large, sunny living-room with a high ceiling and a picture rail; a neat galley kitchen; two good-sized bedrooms and a bathroom. It is 570 square feet, the estate agent tells us. I glance at Karim. That is about half the size of my house in Dublin. All the walls are painted white, and the hall, living-room and bedrooms have new grey carpet. As we move from room to room, Karim is growing more excited. He asks the estate agent about the heating system, the service charge, parking. In the bedroom, he smiles at me and raises his eyebrows.

—Nice, isn't it? he says.

—Yes, I say, looking out the window at the rooftops and windows of other buildings.

—It's a decent size, too, he says. And the price is good. We could afford it if we sold your house in Dublin.

I stand alone in the middle of the living-room and try to imagine myself here. A sofa along this wall. A coffee table. Bookshelves. I try to picture my books here. All the books in my life, untouched at home for a long time now. Poetry, fiction, essays, biography, all mixed up, and yet I could, in an instant, put my hand on any book I wanted. I am separated from them all now. I look around this bare, soulless room. What would I do here all day? I would be far from home, among strangers. I think of Karim's sister and Aisha and the women in the park and in the mosque. I miss Elaine, and Sinéad, and my teaching colleagues. I think of my father and mother at home in Galway, and I have a vision of future Christmases, my mother lifting the turkey out of the oven, Fintan and Elaine and their partners all around the table set with lighting candles, and me here in this flat, in my hijab, on Christmas morning, standing, kneeling, bowing down in prayer.

I can hear Karim talking to the estate agent in the hall, and I am frightened at how far I have come, and how much of myself I have left behind.

33

—I CAN'T DO this any more, I tell Karim.

He hits the mute button on the TV. Do what? he asks.

—Everything. This life . . . Islam . . . It's too much. I can't live like this any more.

He closes down his laptop. What are you talking about, Melina?

—I miss my old life. I miss my family, my friends. I miss my books and going to films. I feel impoverished. There's just so much that's haram – so much you tell me is haram. I point to the garden. Look at Boo, I say, outside in all kinds of weather.

—She has a kennel, he snaps, as he stands up. And there's nothing stopping you from seeing your family and friends – or from reading books, so long as they're not full of filth.

—I cannot remember when I last laughed, when I last felt *happy*. I look at him, pleading. I feel no joy, Karim. There's no joy in Islam for me any more.

—Do you know what you're saying? This is apostasy! You know the punishment for turning your back on Islam? You will go to hell!

—Well, I'll have company there, won't I? Because everyone I know will be there. My poor, innocent father and mother will be there. Do they deserve that, Karim? What terrible sins have they committed? My voice starts to break.

—Anna, please, come here. He puts his hands out to me.

—Where is the compassion, Karim? Isn't compassion more important than belief?

—You're a good Muslim, Anna. You're just going through a time of doubt. We all have those times – I do too. It will get easier, I promise. Please, listen to me. Your punishment, if you turn your back on Islam, will be *so* great I cannot bear to think of it.

Through the window I see Boo mooching around the garden. I no longer know what to do, or what is right or wrong. Boo turns and looks in the window straight at me, and I bury my face in Karim's shoulder.

He makes a great effort from this on. When I enter the room he switches from Al Jazeera to RTÉ or BBC. At the weekend, we go for long walks and drives in Wicklow. He brings me little gifts and reminds me of our good fortune, of all that Allah has given us. He shows me the surahs in the Qur'an which detail the rewards that the faithful will receive on Judgment Day, and those that list the punishments that apostates will suffer in the grave. Daily, hourly, my state of mind fluctuates: I swerve from hope and optimism at the thought of returning to my old life to paralysing fear that I will be struck down if I abandon Allah. Alone, I cry. Karim is a *good* man, he has done nothing wrong. And Islam has brought me feelings of gratitude, benevolence, harmony with the universe;

it has given me a system by which I can live a good life, a code by which I can become a better person.

But nothing seems right any more; everything is in turmoil. When Karim is in Cork for an IT conference one weekend, I deliberately neglect my prayers. I bring Boo inside and it is like old times. In the evening, as I cook dinner, I put on *The Köln Concert*, then *Astral Weeks*. How can this music and these lyrics, which evoke such sublime feeling, be haram? Do not music and art express the divine? Later, I watch TV and laugh out loud at a stand-up comedian. On Saturday, I go to an exhibition at IMMA and walk around the rooms, as if newly liberated. In the basement café, I order lunch and a glass of red wine. I take out *The Waste Land*, and eat and drink and read until the words and the wine inebriate me and I arrive at a bright and new-found clarity. I walk out into the late afternoon, light-headed, and stroll towards the city centre to get the bus home.

—It's not just Islam, I say, on Sunday evening. It's us, too — you and me. We've come to the end.

Karim is on the sofa, working on his laptop. He takes off his headphones.

—I'm sorry, Karim. You know, in your heart, it hasn't been good between us for a long time. I pause, unable to say that it's been six months since we made love.

—Melina, he says softly. We've been over this. It's just a phase you're going through.

—It's not a phase, Karim. It's over . . . You have to leave.

—This is apostasy, he says, angry now. I told you. To come to Islam, to accept Allah and then deliberately turn your back on Him — this is the worst sin for a Muslim. He gives me a long hard look. You would be lost without me, he says.

—Lost without you? Really? Because you're a perfect Muslim, Karim? You've been living and sleeping with me, all this time. What's that sin called? What does the Qur'an say about fornication, Karim? And hypocrisy?

He is furious. I'm trying to save you, he says. You'll regret this. Then he puts his headphones back on.

—It's over, Karim. You have to go.

But he is already tapping the keys of his laptop, ignoring me.

Day by day, I try to wean myself off Islam but, fearful of God's retribution and feeling guilty about Karim, I waver in my resolve. How can I turf him out? Where will he go?

He is sleeping in the back bedroom now, and we go on as normal. In the evenings we eat together, on Saturdays we shop together. The longing to be free never leaves me, but every time I bring up the subject, Karim puts on the headphones. You'd be lost without me, he says.

I get up in the middle of the night to go to the bathroom. The light is on in his room, and I see from the moving shadows that he is praying. I lie awake until dawn. I need help to extricate myself from Karim and Islam. Without help, I will go on living this secret life.

34

IN A DREAM, I am flying over New York City.

I am flying. There is no plane. I have wings.

Below, Manhattan's street grid.

I soar above sunlit roofs and trees and cars, and there is no limit to all my heart can hold.

From the Irish directory of psychoanalysts, I select a member who describes herself as a Jungian. On the phone, Christina O'Connor-Thompson tells me she is almost seventy, and is no longer taking on new clients. She names a male colleague she can recommend. But I persist. I am a follower of Jung, I tell her, I have studied him all my life, I've kept a dream journal for years. I am reluctant to work with a male therapist, I say, because transference issues might slow progress.

—Call me Chris, she says, when I take a seat in a book-lined room in her ground-floor apartment not far from the sea in Blackrock. She is tall and slim with short white hair – an Irish bluestocking – and I like her instantly. As a young woman, she studied English literature at Trinity College and later moved to Switzerland, where she lived for thirty-eight years. After gaining her postgraduate degree in Basel University, she became interested in Jung and switched her studies to psychoanalysis. She married a Swiss man, who she later divorced. She has one daughter who lives in Rome with her husband and son. Four years ago, Chris returned to Ireland because, she says, this country is kinder to old people.

—So. What are the dreams serving up these days? she asks.

I tell her about the New York dream. I was free of everything, of all entanglements. It was pure heaven.

—What does New York mean to you? she asks. What does it represent in your psyche?

—Freedom. Opportunity. Endless possibilities. I know the reality can be different, I know all the pitfalls, but . . . I've always loved New York – I spent a summer there when I was a student. I used to fantasise about living there.

—And now?

I laugh. I'm too old now.

—I'm not aware of any age restrictions for residents of New York.

I see Chris every Thursday evening. We talk about books and writers and each other's lives. On her bookshelves, the sight of authors I recognise from my own shelves – Barbara Hannah, Melanie Klein, Anna Akhmatova, Czesław Miłosz – brings a surge of happiness. I recall a line from Miłosz, *Crippled leaves and dust,* and share it with Chris.

—This is what I love about Jungian therapy, I say, this openness, this collaboration and mutual sharing.

I tell her about Peter, our marriage, the pregnancies, his death. About meeting Karim. I read her the dream from years ago — of being in Harold's Cross Park and getting the phone call from Ahmad.

Then I brace myself.

—I am a Muslim, I say. For three years, I've been a Muslim. I shake my head. Sweet Jesus, a *Muslim*! I get up every night, put on a hijab and pray.

What were, only yesterday, occasions of fear and anxiety, now appear almost comical. I tell Chris about praying at my parents' house and flinging off the hijab when I hear my mother's footsteps on the stairs. Sitting there in Chris's sunny, tranquil room in Blackrock, it is as if I am talking about someone else's life.

—My problem, I say, or *one* of my problems is that I'm easily swayed by other people's ideas and opinions, believing them to be superior to my own. It even happens in school, with colleagues. I'm not even conscious when it's happening . . . I'm embarrassed admitting this, even to myself, but somehow I'm frequently unable to keep myself separate — I'm liable to fuse with anyone or anything.

Chris nods. Go on, she says.

—In another era, I might have joined a religious order.

—Oh yes, you could've been the ideal nun, Chris says.

I smile. It's not that I want to be told what to do, I say, but I long for a simple life; I long to be free of all the outer chaos. I sometimes think if I'd grown up in America, I might have joined a cult! I was always a follower. Certainly, when I was younger, I'd have been prone. I'd have to be deprogrammed if I ever got out!

—A little like what you're doing now? Chris asks, with a wry smile.

I give her a quizzical look.

—Do you need to be deprogrammed from Islam?

—Perhaps. I never thought of it like that.

—But you're right, she says. You *are* porous . . . permeable. And you're susceptible to the numinous too.

—Mmm . . . That'll be my excuse if I ever have to explain my conversion. Susceptible to the numinous.

I look out the window at the communal garden with shrubs and flowers.

—There's a Derek Mahon poem, I say, called 'The Mute Phenomena', in which he says that everything – all matter – is susceptible.

She gives a little clap. I know Derek, she exclaims. We were students together in Trinity. Actually, we dated for a while, she says mischievously.

—You're joking!

—I think I was too tall for him, she says with a chuckle.

In the silence that falls between us then, I try to recall lines from the Mahon poem. Something about the sex lives of cutlery, and the revolutionary theories advanced by turnips. *God is alive and lives under a stone.* And the final lines. *Already in a lost hubcap is conceived the ideal society which will replace our own.* I have missed poetry, words and images like these that take me to the very heart of matter.

On the drive back along the coast road, I feel exhilarated. The world is radiant again – the streets, the trees, the pavements, the people. Then, when I turn onto my street and see Karim's car outside the house, my heart sinks, and my confidence starts to crumble.

35

THE DREAMS FLOW again and, week after week, I bring them to Chris. There's a burglar in my house, I'm being chased by a criminal down a dark alley. Ah-ha, your Shadow, Chris exclaims. I'm sitting, semi-naked, at a teachers' meeting. I have committed murder and am terrified I'll be found out. There's a great catastrophe – the end of the world, Judgment Day perhaps – and everyone is fleeing, and I am driving along the old road to Galway. Somewhere near Kinnegad, I see Peter, up ahead, cycling towards me. As soon as he recognises me, he turns into a field and cycles in a wide arc to avoid me. So great a sinner am I that even Peter Gallagher avoids me.

—I'm afraid, I tell Chris, that without Karim in my life, without his influence and the influence of Islam, I will be *less good*. That I'll lose some aspect or essence of goodness that I learned while I was with him . . . Oh, I have so many fears these days.

Chris takes a few moments to reply.

—You mentioned, before, your tendency to project onto others, especially men, and that's natural, we all project onto others at times – wisdom, authority, intelligence. But, remember, you have your own agency. You're not dependent on anyone – father, mother, lover – to empower you. But I understand your fear. Can we talk about that – what are you most afraid of?

—God's retribution . . . That I'll be struck down. I know how crazy that sounds. Jesus! It's the twenty-first century. I'm an educated woman. I believe in science. I know, rationally, that listening to music or reading literature or drinking a glass of wine is not sinful. And yet I've willingly deprived myself of these pleasures. And I feel weighed down, burdened all the time.

—What is it that burdens you?

—Islam, I whisper, as if I might be heard – as if God might hear me, or see my tongue moving, denigrating Islam.

—What specifically, in Islam?

—So many things . . . The thought of fasting for Ramadan every year for the rest of my life depresses me. As soon as Ramadan ends, I start to dread the next Ramadan, even though it's eleven months away. That's no way to live.

—What else?

—I allowed Karim to put Boo outside in a kennel because he says Islam forbids a dog in the house.

Chris nods. Is she still outside?

—No, I took her in. Karim just avoids being in the same room as her now.

—Anything else?

—The secrecy. This secret life I'm living . . . I feel like I'm suffocating. You know, I didn't go to my old school reunion last year because it happened during Ramadan and I was fasting.

I lied, I said I had a family wedding that weekend . . . I'm lying to everyone. I'm deceiving my family. And now I'm starting to keep secrets from Karim.

—Like what?

—I had a drink when I was out with the school staff last weekend. And I haven't told him I'm seeing you.

—Why not?

—I don't know . . . He'll think I'm disloyal. He'll feel deceived. And I *am* deceiving him, I'm going behind his back.

—Are you? Therapy is a private matter. There's a difference between deception and privacy.

—Also, if I tell him . . . then he'll really know the end is coming.

—And you want to spare him from this knowledge?

I shrug. I know it's not my business to save him from suffering, I say, but I hate hurting him. Karim and Islam are bound together, inextricably linked.

I pause and look out the window. A black cat moves along the grass near the wall. Karim loves cats – whenever we come upon one in the street, he stops and strokes it. Now I remember all his sweetness, his sincerity. The little boy who shared his treats with his poor classmates. His lonely teenage years in Paris, his collapse on the Métro. His grief for Youssef.

—Karim is a good man, Chris, a kind man. He's done nothing wrong. He hasn't cheated on me. He's not a drunk, or violent. I start to cry. Is this what we do now when we fall out of love – we just discard people?

—This is more than falling out of love, isn't it? Chris asks softly. And you're right – Karim is a good, kind man.

—And I'm about to put him out on the street.

—Relationships break down all the time. And, by the way, one doesn't need to be grateful to a man for being faithful, Anna, or for not being drunken or violent. And, well, I'm no expert but, from everything you've said, I think that Karim's interpretation and practice of Islam is . . . quite strict.

I nod. I have been reluctant to admit this, even to myself.

—The question is: Is life with Karim tenable for you?

I shake my head.

—Karim is a grown man, with a career and a good income, Chris says. He'll find a place to live. He'll get on with his own life. Have you thought that maybe you're doing him a disservice by pitying him?

—Here with you, every week, I feel strong, and more confident about giving up Islam and Karim. But when I get home, I slip back, plagued, again, by doubts. It's like I'm still hedging my bets. What if Islam is right? I can only say this to you, Chris, but I am *haunted* by the thought of Judgment Day, haunted by the punishment in the grave. And I feel guilty that I haven't told my parents about Islam, in case Karim is right and it's all true and non-believers really will go to hell. I know it's crazy to think like this. I cannot help it. I'm afraid all the time.

I reach for a tissue.

—You're in the grip of a complex, Anna, she says. It's like all complexes – they blind us. The complex wants to keep you unconscious. And – you know this – you know that Judgment Day is a metaphor, a symbol. It's not meant to be understood literally.

—I know all that, Chris, and I understand it all *intellectually*. I do! But . . . I cannot help it. Apostasy is the greatest sin in

Islam, and I *feel* it as a sin . . . And because I'm planning to leave Islam, I feel doomed and endangered all the time now.

Chris takes some time before speaking again.

—You know from reading Jung, she says, that individuation – the journey of becoming conscious – is painful. One has to relinquish much of the old life, so there's a great sense of loss. It feels like a death. And it *is* a death of sorts. This is one of the reasons you're so frightened and uncertain. Islam has been a home to you for several years. You were drawn to it at a vulnerable time in your life. You'd lost a child – and that was a particularly terrifying experience, a very *primal* experience physically and mentally – it was almost annihilating. Then your marriage ended, and your husband was killed far from home – and his body was never found. Islam offered you safety and security and a degree of psychic order and stability after these traumas. It became a haven. It gave you meaning for a while, and a system – clear rules you could follow – that provided order and routine and discipline. It also offered a philosophy, and a way of life that teaches peace and kindness and humility – and all of this appealed to you . . . You're a God-minded person, Anna, and idealistic in nature, and wanting to live a life of submission and humility is what people have been attracted to down through the ages – the call to religious life. And Islam *is* all of those things – it has goodness and beauty, it shares the same tenets as other religions: do unto others . . . and love thy neighbour. But it is, as you know, flawed, like all religions, and full of dogma and rigid, man-made rules . . . You've been depriving yourself of the joys of art and culture. You've been starved of these riches and the meaning they gave you. I've never studied Islam closely, but I very much doubt it's meant to be interpreted so narrowly and prohibitively. At any rate, you've been — your own word — *impoverished*. You can allow art and literature and music — and the pleasures you've always enjoyed — back into your life again, Anna. And in doing so, you don't have to give up God. Belief or unbelief is a private matter. No group or sect has a monopoly on God. And as for fearing His retribution . . . well, I think that, by degrees, as you become more conscious, your fears will dissipate.

In the ensuing silence, a sense of peace and understanding falls on me.

—I wake in the middle of the night sometimes, and I ask myself: How did I become this weak and helpless, this . . . *foolish*? I can never tell anyone else about this secret life. I'd be so ashamed.

—Do you still think you're helpless?

—No.

—What is it you'd be ashamed of?

—That I let this happen. That I was so submissive . . . That I didn't have more backbone and stand up to Karim, and say — I don't know — say *Oh, come on!* Like, for instance, when he told me angels won't enter the house with Boo there. Angels! Jesus Christ, if anyone heard me. Or when I believed that reading Nabokov was haram. I don't understand it — how did I let this happen?

—My impression is that you weren't passive, that you didn't *let this happen.* I think you were on a quest. You sought a meaningful life, like anyone on a spiritual quest. You educated yourself about Islam, you read the scholars, you were drawn to its beauty and purity. And you love to study, you're a seeker of knowledge — it's who you are. So, for the most part, Islam, like any religion or philosophy, gave you meaning for a while. So don't be too hard on yourself.

I have a sudden vision of sitting with Elaine, and telling her I am a Muslim. And the look of incomprehension on her face. Her speechlessness. The reality of this life is so far beyond everyone's ken.

—Jesus, Chris, amn't I lucky I never went as far as wearing the hijab in public? Can you imagine – walking into school every morning? The look on people's faces! Parents, teachers, the kids . . . I'd be mortified now. How would I ever have come back from that?

Chris nods. I've thought of that too, she says. But there's no shame in wearing the hijab.

After a while, we grow quiet and serious again.

—You know, lately, I've been thinking, wondering . . . if, all my life, perhaps I've given too much precedence to the inner life, to the detriment of my relationships? Wanting all that solitary time to myself – reading, thinking, turning inwards – maybe I neglected those around me. Or, at least, I didn't pay enough attention. Maybe Peter sensed this. And then, later, by embracing Islam, I was doing the same, turning inwards.

—You mean you lacked balance between the inner and outer dimensions of your life?

—Yes, that my life was – is – lopsided. And quite selfish, too, if you think about it. I've always managed to ring-fence my solitude, above all else . . . Chris, maybe I *unconsciously* chose men – Peter, Karim – who were unavailable at some level? Peter was absent physically, he was always away, and when he was there he was mentally unreachable. And Karim was somewhat unreachable too . . . certainly, culturally. What

I'm saying is that this absence suited me — it freed me up to have my solitude. I don't mean that these were deliberate *choices* on my part, but that maybe I was acting, unconsciously, out of self-preservation.

—Yes, I think that's an important observation, Anna.

—It *was* self-preservation for me, you know? I can withstand almost anything — and I *did* tolerate things I shouldn't have tolerated — but I think I'd die without my solitude . . . Peter might have damaged my body, but he didn't take my mind. No one can take my mind.

—Indeed. You're entitled to live your life as you please. Millions of people pursue the life of the mind. And within relationships, too. Was it Rilke who defined love as two solitudes that protect and border each other?

Now, a new, troublesome thought surfaces.

—If we follow this line of thinking — that I unconsciously protected my inner space — then . . . I never really wanted a child, did I? I never wanted that burden of responsibility. A child would have taken up all the space in my head.

—Go on.

—Did my own unconscious *prevent* me from having a child, Chris? Is that what happened? Did my unconscious spare me and, in the process, a child died? A child was sacrificed?

—Unconscious forces — including those in the personal unconscious — can, as you know, be very powerful. However, what might *seem* like a negative occurrence — or even a tragedy — to us, *rationally*, might, in the whole scheme of things, be viewed in another, less negative manner.

—Do you mean viewed from outside or *beyond* the rational? In a metaphysical sense?

—Yes, exactly. Do you think, for a moment, you could view your child's death from a metaphysical perspective?

—From the perspective of his soul?

Chris nods. Yes. And yours too.

My heart and mind start to race. Perhaps it was not just I who was spared. Perhaps the child himself was spared this life, this suffering. The right thing may have happened.

—Any dreams this week? Chris asks, before the end of our session.

—None that I can remember. But there's an old dream that still haunts me – the Harold's Cross Park dream I told you about at the start.

—Yes, I remember. In Jungian terms, that was a big dream.

—I'm still shaken by the fact that, two years before I ever set eyes on Karim, my unconscious *foretold* him in that dream. My psyche foretold that something significant – Islam – was imminent. And it was a positive dream; it seemed to sanction, even *bless*, my relationship with Karim and with Islam . . . So, you see, if I give up Islam and Karim, am I not defying my own psyche, rejecting what my unconscious deemed for me? You see why I'm so afraid? It's like I'm going against my own destiny.

Chris is pensive then. You're right, she says, your unconscious did predict your encounter with Islam and signalled it would be significant and positive. And spiritually, mentally, intellectually, Islam was an important part of your individuation, Anna. This part of your life need not be denied or viewed as a negative or shameful experience. But now, there's another shift occurring in your unconscious, and you're moving on.

But that doesn't mean that Islam wasn't the right thing for you *at that time*. And, importantly, this psychic shift you're currently undergoing is being done consciously – you're not blindly stumbling out of Islam into another complex. . . Psychologically, you're very healthy, very resilient. She pauses for a moment. The journey of individuation is lifelong. There's always more work to be done – there's no such thing as being too conscious – so we'll always face new challenges. But remember, nothing is ever wasted.

36

KARIM IS SHAKING his head.

—You don't need a therapist, Melina, he says. You have Allah.

—We have to part, Karim. I'm sorry, you have to leave.

Without another word, he goes to the hall, picks up his gym bag and heads out the door.

All evening long, I wait anxiously for his return. Finally, after nine o'clock, I hear his key in the door. He goes straight up to his room. In the middle of the night, I wake with a feeling of prescience, and a faint echo in my ears, as if someone is calling or crying. I think, immediately, it is Peter calling me. I lie very still, listening out, but the house is silent. I close my eyes and long for sleep but I am in the grip of fear and doom again.

At dawn I get up. Boo is stretched out on her bed in the kitchen. She lifts her head feebly, and gives a faint wag of her tail, but something is wrong. When I lift her in my arms, she moans. Then Karim comes into the room.

—What's wrong? he asks.

—I don't know. She's not well. I'm going to take her to the vet.

—I'll drive you, he says.

—No, I'll manage.

Richard, the vet, examines her carefully, gently.

—She's a very ill little dog, he says. It might be something she ate, or something else. He looks at her chart. She's ten, almost eleven, right? And her last bloods showed her liver function is low.

He strokes her head. He has known Boo since she was a puppy.

—We'll admit her and do bloods first and that'll give us an idea. We may need to do further tests, but nine times out of ten, it's an infection or something they ate. We'll put her on a drip and get antibiotics into her. I'll give you a call at lunchtime.

As soon as I get into the car, I break down. I drive down the canal to Sandymount and walk along the strand. It is Saturday, not yet 10 a.m. The air is cool and the tide is far out. Peter and I used to bring Boo here when she was a puppy, before everything fell apart. She'd run in wide circles around us on her little legs, egging us on for a chase. Then we'd run after her and laugh at the way the wind pinned her ears back. No words for such joy then. Now, I walk far out on the empty beach and sit on the damp sand. It was Boo, not Peter, calling during the night. And I didn't rise and go to her. She's lying in the vet's surgery now, in the midst of powerful new smells and sounds that frighten her, straining to stay conscious. I close my eyes, and pray. Sacred heart of Jesus, I place all my trust in thee. La ilaha illa Allah, Mohammedur rasoolu Allah.

Richard calls me at lunchtime.

—The bloods are back, he says, and the news isn't good, I'm afraid. She has liver disease . . . It's well advanced. This isn't what you want to hear, or what I expected.

I am standing at the kitchen sink. On the other side of the window, I can see the asphalt roof of her kennel. Upstairs, Karim is moving about his room, packing.

—She's on a drip but she's quite weak, Richard says. The prognosis is not good. He pauses, waiting for my response. It can be very rapid, he continues. Sometimes . . . a matter of days.

I grit my teeth, then bite down on my knuckles.

—A blood transfusion may help, Richard says. It can buy a little time. If that's something you want to consider.

—Yes, I say, give her the transfusion.

That evening, Richard carries her into the treatment room, and as soon she sees me, she struggles in his arms to reach me. He places her on the table and she wags her tail and licks the tears on my face and I put my arms around her, and rest my head gently against her neck.

Richard is silent, and solemn.

—The transfusion has given her a lift, and some energy, he says. But she's very sick. We'll see how the night goes.

Just after ten o'clock, I get a call from the vet on night duty. Boo has deteriorated in the last hour.

When I arrive, he brings her out and places her gently on

a blanket on the table. Her eyes are closed. She's no longer conscious. Every few seconds, her whole body jerks. I kiss her head, her eyes. When I leave my hand on her chest, a trickle of blood flows from her mouth onto the blanket. I look at the vet in panic.

He nods slowly. I'm very sorry, he says. I think it's time.

He leaves me alone with her to say my goodbyes.

I lay my head on the blanket beside hers, and kiss her forehead.

I whisper her name.

—I'm sorry, I say.

Then the vet enters and draws the pink liquid into the syringe and, after a few minutes, she dies in my arms.

37

A TREMENDOUS SIGHT . . . Camus wrote, as he sailed into New York Harbour in March 1946. *Order, power, economic strength, they're all here. The heart trembles before such remarkable inhumanity.* During the three months he spent here, Camus seemed especially vulnerable. He was often beset with illness and feelings of melancholy, homesickness, an inability to fit in. He found the city at times menacing, and was unnerved by the enormous wealth. But he admired the women on the streets and the colour of the taxis, and he appreciated American hospitality and cordiality and, one day on a bus, he witnessed an ordinary white American giving up his seat to an older Black woman.

I rise at 7 a.m. and take the lift down to the foyer and cross 91st Street to The Vinegar Factory, one of a cluster of upmarket food emporiums owned by Eli Zabar. Everything is delicious and costs the earth, but I cannot resist. I take coffee and an almond croissant back upstairs and watch NY1 city news. My apartment is on the fifth floor of a building on the corner of York Avenue and 91st Street, and comes with two cats, Geoffrey and Fiona, whose owner, Jennifer, has swapped her home for mine in Dublin. All day long, the cats sit on the windowsill gazing out at the brick wall of the building next door, primed for any sign of movement. When a bird lands on the window ledge, inches away, their bodies stiffen as the near-dormant stalking instinct is resurrected. Geoffrey is the shy one; when I first arrived, he was missing for hours, hidden behind the kickboard of a kitchen cabinet. In contrast, Fiona shoots past my head when I enter and comes skidding to a halt on the kitchen counter, purring loudly and demanding attention. Last week she walked across my lap, stepped on the remote control and scrambled the TV channels. Yep, I told Fintan on the phone, I had to call the Cable Guy.

Mid-morning, I switch on the radio or browse Sunday's *New York Times*, then clean the litter trays, and take out the trash. It is when I cross the landing and drop the trash into the chute that I feel most like a New Yorker, the woman I've longed to be, a woman with ease and confidence and a God-free state of mind. But, in the afternoon, when I walk around the streets, into the cold shadow of a skyscraper one minute and bright sunlight bouncing off glass the next, the old disquiet returns, and I know well I am no New Yorker, I know well who I am.

On Fridays I find myself gravitating towards the mosque on 3rd Avenue as Muslims gather for Jum'ah prayer. Sitting in a nearby café, I am flooded with a rapid crescendo of memories and images: a procession of Allah's names, still coming, unbidden, in increments of four; the muezzin's call to prayer that moved Camus at eighteen; the little girl fleeing her bulldozed home in the West Bank with the basin of utensils. The sorrow in Karim's voice when he said, You're tired of me, aren't you? I still recite the Shahada in times of fear. I still discard my nail clippings into plant pots and use my right hand to eat and, on arrival in a new place, mentally orient myself towards Mecca, as if I still mean to pray. I came across the Korean word, han, the other day. It has no English equivalent, but it evokes loss and resentment, sorrow and grief. And the feeling of being less than whole. I thought of Camus too. There is no escaping han.

I keep track of Karim on LinkedIn. He's living in Paris now, working with an international IT solutions company. From the reflected light behind him, his photograph appears to have been taken near water. He is wearing a blue shirt and a dark jacket, and has a black bag slung over his shoulder. His hair is still dark and he has that shy, endearing smile that still arrests me. When I zoom in, I see he has a prayer mark on his forehead, the sign of long hours spent in worship. I search the foreground for a shadow or some indication of who took this photo. I would like, one day, to come upon a photograph of him with a woman, a Muslim wife.

I saw him once, a few months after he left. I was waiting at the bus stop near my house when I recognised the figure coming along the footpath, his gym bag on his shoulder. I smiled as he drew near, and said his name, but he walked right past me without a word. I emailed him that evening, hurt and upset, and accused him of heartlessness. *I'm sorry*, he replied, *I got a shock seeing you, I couldn't speak. Please, Melina, I beg you, return to Islam. Go back to God. I cry when I remember how you used to get up in the dark for Fajr prayer. You were such a good Muslim. Have you forgotten — the adhan can be heard on the moon?*

I had the thought this morning that it is possible to warp one's own character by submitting to authority. *Warp* was the word that came to mind. Then, instead of thinking how this idea might manifest in myself, instead of exploring how my character might be warped, I immediately thought of its antonym. It's time you straightened yourself out, I thought, with a smile.

Tonight, the president-elect was waving at a crowd when my phone rang. At the sound of my mother's voice, I put the TV on mute. Elaine and her two children are at home with my parents while her husband is travelling for work. There's nothing on the news here, she said, but the banking crisis.

—Your father hasn't been feeling great, she said then, and my stomach did a somersault. Dr Brennan referred him on to a consultant. He had a CT scan on Monday and some abnormality is showing up in the lung . . . He has to go in next week for a biopsy.

There is not a day that goes by when I am not grateful for my childlessness. When strangers pass me on the streets, I am reminded of Eliot's crowd flowing over London Bridge and I think, Can one be this light and unencumbered all the time? Lately I've thought about writing to Peter, as if he still existed. There is still much to say. *Your DNA is in me, Peter,* I would write, *hidden deep in my cells. Did you know that? Did you know that our child's cells mixed with mine to form a minute organism that will never leave me?* If he had lived, the child would be thirteen now, about to enter puberty. His name would be Andrew. In my mind, he is a quiet, pale boy; brown-haired, more like me, physically, than Peter. Troubled, somehow. A fatherless boy. Or maybe not. Maybe, in that alternate life, Peter does not fall to his death in a far-off land. Or maybe he falls, but, like Joe Simpson, he makes it up out of the dark crevasse and crawls through a blizzard, being watched by the mountains, if not by God.

Jennifer calls me from Dublin. She hears scratching sounds in the attic at night. She fears rodents, but I assure her it's just birds landing on the roof.

I am disturbed, at times, by the thought of Jennifer in my house, in the rooms that bear traces of me and Boo, and even Karim – our hair or dead skin cells trapped in the floorboards or in folds of fabric, faint decibels of our voices still hovering close to ceilings. Day by day, the house will have adjusted to her presence. She might open a book, whose words were only ever tracked by my eyes, but which will, now, benignly receive hers. She might reach into the bottom of the bookcase and lift out the little terracotta urn containing Boo's ashes, and frown, confounded by the thought of a body that produced so little ash.

I put on my coat and hat and go up on the roof to smoke. Darkness is falling. The lights come on in the Astro pitch across the street where teenagers gather to play soccer. In the distance, the East River. It is not Peter I grieve, or the dead child, or even Youssef gunned down in the street. It is Boo. Boo, banished from the house in her final years on the orders of Karim and God; Boo, in her cold kennel in the dead of winter as the ground froze and snow fell and I slept in my warm bed upstairs. Or standing in the back garden, her small, uncomprehending eyes fixed on my back as I walk away and close the door and turn the key again and again and again. I will carry my betrayal to my grave. I am like Meursault, accused of the wrong crime. It is not the sin of apostasy I should confess, but the sin of cruelty inflicted on an innocent animal.

I consider taking the subway up to Fort Tryon Park, for no other reason than that Camus went there in 1946 when the magnolias were in full bloom. Instead, I stay home and browse a classic car website where, for the princely sum of €48,900, one can purchase a 1959 Facel Vega HK500 – the exact make, model and year of the sports car Michel Gallimard smashed into a tree near Villeblevin on January 4th 1960. Other notable owners of the Facel Vega in the late 1950s and '60s included Pablo Picasso, Ava Gardner and Stirling Moss.

I still obsess about Camus. I spend hours poring over his books, examining photographs, delving into his life. I want to feel, constantly, his proximity, the approach of his fragile self while simultaneously suffering the nausea and weakness – Stendhal syndrome? – that exposure to him induces in me. I am addicted to this sickness. There is a particular photograph taken at the crash scene that brings desolation down on me. It is of a few men, local men perhaps, standing there, struck dumb. And who would not have fallen silent in that spot? In the days before he left his home in Lourmarin for Paris, Camus had written, separately, to three lovers. *I'm arriving Tuesday by car*, he wrote to María Casares. *I'll phone you when I arrive, but maybe we can already set a dinner date for Tuesday. Let's say Tuesday in principle, taking into account surprises on the road . . .*

* * *

Last night I dreamt of my father's funeral. As the cortège paused outside our house, my brother stepped in to shoulder the coffin. This morning, I took a walk on the esplanade by the East River, and met a man with three cats on a leash. There is a need to record everything now: the flower sellers on the corner of 2nd Avenue; the stretch of Madison where the sun dazzles in early morning; the men in white thobes hurrying along 3rd Avenue to Friday prayer.

I can already picture my flight home. It will be night-time and I will settle in with my books and my blanket, and when the plane thunders down the runway, I will hedge my bets and close my eyes and whisper the Shahada. I will remind myself that Camus's death was instant, and Youssef's and Boo's were swift too, and maybe even Floc, the Skye terrier, found a soft spot in which to lie down and die. I will try to think of soft spots, and open fields, and overhanging trees. I will remember that Peter is just a chimera in my body, as Karim is in my soul. Later, when we're at cruising altitude and the cabin goes quiet and the lights flicker off and on, and then off again, I might attain that serene state of consciousness that entry into upper earth often brings. There, Insha'Allah, I will go beyond thought and fear and memory, to where a vision of lightening – the flaring of the spirit before death – gives way to something else, something ongoing, some aftermath, a realm of imaginative possibilities to which I am not, ordinarily, given access.